Take Six Puppies

"Come on, then, little lady," the vet was saying. "What have you got there, then?"

What did he mean? Anna wondered. What could a stray dog have brought with her? She crept closer into the stall now, and peered past Beth's sturdy boots down into the fresh straw.

Nobody noticed her; they were all too busy looking down at the dog. Anna watched too, as the dog lifted her handsome, hound-like head and peered round with moist brown eyes. Not at Anna, though. She was looking at something wriggling in the straw. Two some-things – three. Anna moved even closer and saw that they were tiny puppies!

Other Hippo Animal Stories:

Thunderfoot
Vanilla Fudge
Deborah van der Beek

A Foxcub Named Freedom
Pirate the Seal
Brenda Jobling

Midnight Dancer
Midnight Dancer: To Catch a Thief
Midnight Dancer: Running Free
Midnight Dancer: Fireraisers
Elizabeth Lindsay

Animal Rescue
Bette Paul

HIPPO ANIMAL STORIES

Take Six Puppies

Bette Paul

Hippo

Scholastic Children's Books,
Commonwealth House, 1–19 New Oxford Street,
London WC1A 1NU, UK
a division of Scholastic Ltd
London ~ New York ~ Toronto ~ Sydney ~ Auckland

First published by Scholastic Ltd, 1996

Text copyright © Bette Paul, 1996

ISBN 0 590 13734 4

All rights reserved

Typeset by TW Typesetting, Midsomer Norton, Avon

Printed by Cox & Wyman Ltd, Reading, Berks.

10 9 8 7 6 5 4 3 2 1

Chapter 1

" 'Bye – see you tomorrow!" Anna Bright waved goodbye to her friend, Amy, as the school bus disappeared down the main road. Alone, she turned to walk up Steepy Lane – so steep and narrow that the bus couldn't get up it – to Millington Farm.

After the noise and chatter on the school bus it was very quiet on Steepy Lane, and rather lonely. Anna plodded up the muddy slope with mixed feelings: glad it was home-time, sorry to leave Amy. That was the one thing she didn't like about living way out of the village – she was so far away from her friends. Gloomily she peered up the last bit of slope, and perked up when she saw a big white van parked in the farmyard. Grinning to herself, she broke into a trot.

Beth Johnson's van, she thought. I wonder what she's brought this time!

Beth was the local dog-warden; she collected stray dogs, or pets that people could no longer keep, and brought them to stay at The Millington Dog Sanctuary, until new homes could be found for them. The thought of a new arrival spurred Anna on; she ran faster and faster up the last bit of slope that led straight into the farmyard.

She leaned against the van for a moment, getting her breath back. There were no sounds from the back of the van – no scrabbling or whining. Perhaps Beth had only called to check up on that old collie she'd brought last week? Well, that was one success story anyway, Anna thought – the gentle old dog had been taken in by a gentle old lady down in the village. As usual Anna had been sad to lose the dog even though she knew he was going to a good home. It was one of the things she couldn't get used to.

"Don't get too attached to them," her

mother warned her when they started the sanctuary a year ago. "They're only lodgers here, until we find a new home for them."

"But while they're still here, I can be their friend, can't I?" said Anna.

"Just so long as you don't get too fond of them," her father warned. "We've got quite enough animals of our own without keeping every stray dog in the county!"

He was right, of course, but Anna didn't count the ducks, geese and hens, or the shifting population of sheep and bullocks down in the meadows. She didn't even count Dad's labrador, Rufus, or Mum's tabby-cat, Tabitha. None of them seemed to need her like the stray dogs did. Anna smiled to herself – now it looked as if there would be a new friend for her.

She ran to the kitchen, threw open the door and flung her rucksack inside.

"Mum – what's Beth brought?" she called.

But the kitchen was empty. Only a broad, shaggy dog heaved himself off the doormat and plodded up to her, waving his feathery tail. And a cat purred loudly from somewhere over by the warm stove.

"Hello, Rufus – where is everybody?" She bent to pat the dog's rough yellow coat. In answer, Rufus set off towards the stables, then turned and waited for her to follow.

"Up at the stables, are they?" said Anna. She ran across the farmyard with Rufus, who waited patiently for her to open the stable half-door.

"Mum? Beth? Have you brought a new dog in?" Anna called over the door.

"Shhh!" was the sharp reply – so sharp that Anna knew she'd better obey. Silently, she heaved herself up on the stable door and slid back the bolt. One of the resident strays gave a single bark, another started whining, then a third joined in, snuffling and scrabbling up on his door.

"Quiet!" Beth commanded, and the dogs obeyed immediately.

So did Anna – she slid into the stable and stood up on tiptoe to push the huge iron bolt back in place as quietly as she could. Outside, Rufus started whining and scratching to get in.

"Take Rufus back to the house, Anna," her mother called, softly, this time. "He might upset her."

"Upset who?" Anna asked. She went over to the nearest stall and tried to peer over the half-door but her mother's face suddenly appeared out of the gloom.

"Stray bitch," she said, briefly. "We're just getting her settled in."

"Can I see her?" Anna asked.

"Take Rufus back then wait until Philip arrives – he's due any moment now."

She hadn't answered her question, Anna realized. Well, at least she hadn't said no.

"Come on, Rufus – come on, boy!" She let herself out of the stables, ran back across the yard and straight into the kitchen. Rufus followed her, flopped down beside the cat in front of the stove and watched closely as Anna helped herself from the biscuit tin.

"Sorry, Rufus – you know Dad's rules," she told him. Rufus was very prone to fat; Dad fed him on a very strict dry diet and scraps were forbidden. Anna found this very difficult; she looked at Rufus's pleading brown eyes, and longed to toss him a ginger-nut. Fortunately, before she was too tempted, she heard the sound of a car scrunching across the farmyard.

"That's Philip," she told Rufus. "I'd better go and tell him where to find the new dog."

Philip Weatherby was the local vet. He always gave the strays a check-up when they first arrived – and injections, just to make sure they weren't carrying any disease. So Anna wasn't surprised he was calling just then.

"Hello, Anna!" he said. "Where are these dogs then?"

Anna was puzzled. "There's only one new dog," she said. "Mum and Beth have her up in the bottom stables."

Philip nodded. "I'll get straight along up there." He reached into his Land Rover and took out his medical bag.

"May I come too?" asked Anna.

The vet looked doubtful. "I don't know…" he said.

"Mum said I was to wait for you," Anna told him, truthfully. She couldn't understand his hesitation; she'd watched him check new arrivals before and even when they snarled and growled with fear, she wasn't worried.

Philip Weatherby looked at her. "Oh, all right," he smiled. "You'll do! Lead the way, Nurse Bright!"

Anna led the way up to the stables – approaching silently this time, and standing back to let Philip open the half-door.

"Hello, Laura – oh, and Beth – hi! How's she getting on?" he asked as he passed into the stable.

Getting on with what? Anna wondered. Carefully closing the outer door, she quickly followed Philip into the stall, before anyone could tell her to go away. She needn't have worried: they were all too busy to notice her. Mum and Beth were bending over the bitch and when Philip joined them she heard his usual grunts and mutterings as he apparently examined the dog. But this time it was different.

"Come on, then, little lady," the vet was saying. "What have you got there, then?"

What did he mean? Anna wondered. What

could a stray dog have brought with her? She crept closer into the stall now, and peered past Beth's sturdy boots down into the fresh straw.

Nobody noticed her; they were all too busy looking down at the dog. Anna watched too, as the dog lifted her handsome, hound-like head and peered round with moist brown eyes. Not at Anna, though. She was looking at something wriggling in the straw. Two somethings – three. Anna moved even closer and saw that they were tiny puppies!

"Wow!" Anna breathed softly.

Even as she watched, another one was born. Four pups and a beautiful mother dog – this was better than the single stray she'd been expecting to see! And there was another – five, now! The mother dog turned and licked the latest arrival, who crawled over and snuggled up to her belly.

"Seems you found her just in time," Philip told Beth.

Beth nodded, grimly. "She was hiding out at that old piggery down Stanton way," she said. "I had a report of a stray around there a couple of days ago, but I just couldn't find her. Thought I'd have another look round this afternoon and came across her digging herself in."

"Well, she's managing everything quite well without me," smiled Philip. "I'll just give her the shots and leave her to clean up." He propped his bag on a hay-rack, took out a

syringe and unwrapped it. With a swift movement, he pinched the skin on the dog's neck and plunged the vaccine in. The dog was so busy licking her pups that she never even noticed.

"I'll keep her quiet and warm," said Anna's mum. "They all look quite healthy so far."

"Mother and babies doing well," laughed Beth.

"Come down to the farm and have a cup of tea," said Mrs Bright. "We'll leave this lot in peace for a while."

Anna stepped back into the shadows so nobody noticed her as they left. The outer door clanged and Anna was left alone with the bitch and her five pups.

She didn't quite know why she'd stayed behind: after all, the births were over now and Anna knew the bitch must not be disturbed. Hardly daring to breathe, she stood quite still and watched as the bitch pushed the five pups with her nose until they were all snuggled close against her. One immediately began to suckle, Anna noticed, but the others nuzzled around blindly, squeaking more like kittens than dogs. Anna was longing to help them, but she knew she shouldn't – she'd better go back down to the kitchen, she decided, and leave them all in peace.

Then, just as she was taking a last look at the tiny creatures, she saw the mother dog's flanks heave once more, and suddenly there was another pup in the straw! But this time the animal just lay there, unmoving. And the mother dog didn't even look for it. She was concentrating on pushing all the others into the right positions for feeding. She hadn't even noticed the sixth pup!

Anna watched in horror as the new pup seemed to shake its blind little head, apparently trying to find its way to its mother. But every time it moved a little, its legs gave way and it collapsed in the straw. Anna wanted to pick it up and show it to its mother, but she knew that was dangerous. If she disturbed the bitch she might frighten the pups and their mother would reject them – even kill them to protect them. No, she couldn't possibly risk that – but what should she do?

Philip – that's who she needed! Swiftly,

silently, she slid out of the stall, shutting the half-door firmly, standing on tiptoe to reach the bolt inside. Through the outer door, and down to the farmhouse she ran, faster than she ever knew she could, noting with relief that Philip's Land Rover was still in the yard.

"Philip! Philip!" she called as soon as she was within reach of the kitchen. "Come quickly – there's another puppy!"

"Anna – have you been up at the stables on your own?" her mother asked, sharp as ever.

Anna nodded, leaning against the kitchen door, breathing hard. "I stayed ever so quiet, Mum, just to see the puppies settled but then another was born and it's so tiny..." She stopped, tears already forming in her eyes. "Oh, come on, Philip," she pleaded. "Or you'll be too late!"

"Calm down, Anna," said the vet. "I'll go back up there and see what's to be done."

"I'll come with you," said Anna.

"Not if you're in Philip's way," said Mum.

Philip smiled. "Not Anna," he assured her. "She's a great help in an emergency."

Together, Anna and the vet went back to the stables. This time all five pups were suckling hard, and the mother was happily dozing off. But the sixth pup was still in the straw where she'd left it.

"Hmmmm!" said Philip. "Little runty lad, this one." He bent down, picked up a bundle of straw, and used it to edge the little creature up to its mother's belly. "I don't want to pick him up," he explained. "He'll get my scent on him and the mother might reject him." He stepped back. "She might reject him anyway," he warned Anna. "After all, five's enough for her to feed in her condition."

"But she couldn't just let him die, could she?" asked Anna.

Philip shrugged. "He's a sickly pup, he'll probably die anyway," he said. "I think we're going to have to leave it for her to decide."

He stepped back and Anna could see the runty one now, snuggling feebly up to his mother's belly. She took no notice, just went on sleeping. The runty one nuzzled around a bit, then appeared to fall asleep too. But suddenly he lifted his head and nosed about

again, feebly, vaguely, and, quite by accident, discovered an end teat. But even then he didn't start to suckle.

"Possibly never will," said Philip. "Let's leave him alone to try."

But Anna couldn't bear to leave the tiny animal just then. "He might start to suck," she whispered. "If we tell him..."

Philip smiled and shook his head. "He can't hear us," he said.

"I know," Anna said, impatiently. "I mean, if we just stand here and sort of tell him

silently – like wishing."

"Willing him to feed, you mean?" Philip asked. "Well, it can't do any harm to watch for a while."

Together they stood, in the dim light of the stable, concentrating all their thoughts on this one little animal, a few minutes old, a few moments away from death.

"Please, please, please, little Runty," Anna prayed silently. "Go on, go on…"

And suddenly, with one huge effort, the tiny head lifted, the mouth opened and the little jaws clamped hard on to the mother's teat. Watching closely, Anna was sure she could see the ripple of energy flowing through the tiny body.

"He's feeding!" she whispered.

"Aye, I think he'll do," said Philip. "Though he's bound to be the weakest of the litter."

"Little Runty," smiled Anna. "Well, I'll take special care of him." She smiled fondly down at the little animal, which lay quite still amidst its squirming brothers and sisters.

"Come on, Anna, my tea's getting cold." Philip led the way out of the stables. "You'll have enough to do looking after that lot, without giving special attention to the runt," he told her, once they were outside.

"Oh, I'll manage," Anna assured him, happily.

"Well, at least it won't be for long," said Philip. "In a couple of months they'll all be gone."

A couple of months! Anna couldn't bear to think about it. These were the first puppies to be born at Millington Farm and she wanted to keep them all for ever. Thoughtfully, she followed the vet into the kitchen.

"We ought to be able to find some, given a couple of months," Beth was saying.

"Find what?" asked Anna.

"Homes for those pups," said Beth.

"*Six* homes," groaned Anna's mum. "That won't be easy."

"I'll put an advertisement up in the surgery," said Philip.

"And I'll put one up in the village hall," said Beth.

"And the post office," said Mrs Bright. "And you can put one up at school, Anna."

Anna frowned; she didn't want to do anything that would make the pups leave Millington. "We can't just give them away to anybody," she objected.

"Of course we can't," her mother agreed. "They'll be sold at the proper price, to people who can give them good homes."

"You'll have to meet them first," said Beth. "Ask them round and vet them."

Philip laughed and picked up his bag. "I'll be round in a day or two to check the pups over," he promised. "Don't be surprised if you lose one or two – it's a big litter."

Frowning, Anna watched from the window over the sink as Beth and Philip got into their cars and drove cautiously off down Steepy Lane. Off to advertise our puppies, she thought, sadly. And suddenly a couple of months didn't seem a very long time at all!

Chapter 2

So Anna decided not to tell anyone about the puppies for a while – not even Amy. The pups were her secret and at least for a day or two she didn't want to share them.

Her mother had other ideas.

"Here's the notice about the puppies." She waved a card at Anna one morning at breakfast. "Ask Mrs Parkes if you can pin it on the PTA board today."

"It's a bit soon, isn't it?" asked Anna, secretly dismayed. "I mean, they can't leave their mother for weeks yet."

"And by the time they're ready to leave I want a whole lot of people to be ready to take them," replied her mother, crisply. "The school will be closed for the holidays soon and then nobody will see my advert."

"All right," Anna sighed. "I'll put the notice up today."

So much for her lovely secret!

And, of course, as soon as she showed the notice to Mrs Parkes, everyone in the class knew about the pups.

"Oh, Anna, how lovely!" said Mrs Parkes. "Listen, everybody, Anna has some wonderful news…"

"You didn't tell me," Amy said, as they washed their hands together at break. "Six puppies and you never even mentioned them!"

Amy and Anna usually shared everything – birthday parties, holiday trips, even chicken-pox and mumps! AnnarandAmy, Mr Bright called them, as if they were just one person, which was how they often felt.

Not now, however.

"Why didn't you tell me?" Amy demanded.

"I was going to surprise you in the holidays," said Anna. Well, it was partly the truth – she knew she couldn't keep six puppies a secret once Amy came over to play.

"Oh – I'm dying to see them," said Amy. "Just imagine – six puppies – and I've only ever wanted one!"

"I know," Anna sympathized. "I wish I could give you one."

Amy's parents were out at work all day, and Amy stayed at her Grandma's cottage after school. Grandma Perkins was a great cat lover – she'd never allow a dog into her house. And of course, Amy couldn't leave a puppy at home on its own all day.

"Can I come and play with them at the weekend?" Amy asked.

"Well, we can only peek at them just yet," Anna explained. "They have to be left very quiet for a week or two."

Amy's face fell. "That long?" she said.

"They'll be all right by the Easter holidays," said Anna. "You're coming over then, aren't you?"

"Well – I'll be away for one week," Amy said. "Mum's great London treat, remember?"

Anna nodded – she certainly did remember. She'd been all set to go to London with Amy and her parents until Dad heard how much it was going to cost.

"It's no use, Anna-my-love," he'd said. "What with the rise in feed bills and the building work on the stables, I simply can't afford it."

She'd been terribly disappointed at the time, but now, with the arrival of the six puppies, she was glad she wasn't going away with Amy.

"I expect you'll have sold them all before I get back," said Amy, gloomily.

"Well, you'll be able to help feed and clean them out for several weeks before they leave."

"Great!" Amy cheered up. "Now shall I make a properly printed advertisement on the class computer? It'll attract more attention than your mum's little note."

Amy was mad on computers, she could write and draw and design and could beat the boys in the class in most games. So, once Mrs Parkes had given them the go-ahead, Amy opened up the program while Anna read through the advert her mum had written.

"I'll make a nice bold heading," Amy

decided. And she typed *FOR SALE* at the top of the screen.

"That sounds like a house or a car," Anna protested. "I think we should say 'Good Homes Wanted' like Mum's written here."

She read out the message and watched it appear on the screen as Amy typed:

GOOD HOMES WANTED
For six cross-bred puppies at
Millington Farm Dog Sanctuary
Mother collie-cross.
Father unknown.
Healthy, happy puppies,
White, black and tan.
3M. 3F. Ready end of April.
Only caring owners need apply.

"How will you know whether they're caring or not?" said a voice behind them. The two girls turned and saw the new boy, Danny Forester, waiting for his turn at the computer. Danny rarely spoke to anyone, so they were quite startled for a moment. Then Anna smiled at him.

"Oh, you can tell," she assured him. "The way they handle the pups and the questions they ask. If Mum has any doubts she goes to see their house."

"Like adopting a baby," Danny commented.

"Well, they are only babies, you know," said Anna. "We have to make sure they go to someone who can care for them properly – that's why we're a registered Dog Sanctuary."

Danny Forester nodded thoughtfully as he watched Anna adding the Millington Farm telephone number to the bottom of the advert. Danny was new to Millington Primary – new to life in the country, too. He'd recently moved to an isolated cottage a few miles away so he'd had no chance to make any village friends. And he didn't seem to be making any in school either, Anna had noticed. He was in AnnarandAmy's group in class, but he didn't really belong; he just got on with his work on his own and when he'd finished he'd sit quietly watching the others, just as he was watching Amy now.

Amy pulled the paper out of the printer. "There, it's ready to pin up."

"It's a bit small," said Anna, disappointed. "Nobody will see it on the board amongst all the school notices."

"You could mount it on card with some pictures of the puppies around it," suggested Danny.

"Great idea!" said Anna. "Can you draw puppies, Amy?"

"Not on this computer," said Amy, sadly.

Anna turned to Danny. "Hey – you did those wonderful badgers for the wildlife poster, didn't you?" she said.

"Yes, I did," said Danny, blushing. "I'm quite good at drawing."

"Brill!" said Anna. "Will you do some puppies for us?"

Danny looked pleased. "Of course – have you got any card?" he asked.

That afternoon the three of them worked together: Amy tried out different lettering and fonts on the printer, Anna cut and measured card, and Danny drew six puppy heads.

"What do they look like?" he asked Anna, as he sorted out some pencil-crayons.

"Oh – patchy, I suppose," she said. "Some are white with tan patches, some are brown with white patches – and bits of black here and there." She thought hard for a moment. "Oh – there's one that's black all over and one of them is smaller than the others," she said, remembering little Runty. "His face is all white, his eyes are big and shiny black, and he has a black head and ears."

Danny nodded and drew in the last puppy at the bottom corner of the card, with a little face and huge, appealing eyes. He reached for the crayons and coloured one feathery ear shiny black.

"That's just like Runty!" said Anna.

"Oh – you've given them names then?"

"Not all of them," said Anna, hastily. "It's just this one. He was the last to be born, he's the smallest and the weakest – the runt of the litter."

"I know how he feels," murmured Danny.

Anna looked sideways at him and smiled. Danny was the smallest person in the class, shorter than even the youngest girl and so quiet he was often overlooked. At playtime he didn't join in the hurly-burly games but stood shivering on the side-lines, watching AnnarandAmy and the others racing around playing football. He didn't even join them on the school bus because his mum always picked him up and whisked him off in her little car up the hill away from the village. He must be quite lonely up there, Anna suddenly thought; at least she had all the farm animals to keep her busy.

"Have you got a dog?" Anna asked.

Danny shook his head. "Mum says we can't have any pets until we – get sorted out," he said. He closed his lips firmly, as if to stop himself saying anything more. Scenting a mystery, Anna looked at him with interest but he bent his head and went on colouring patches on the puppies.

"Is it ready?" asked Amy, satisfied at last with her masterpiece of design. She produced her paper from the printer with a flourish. "There – that's quite striking, isn't it?"

"It'll be even more striking when it's mounted on Danny's picture," said Anna. "Everyone's bound to notice it."

"I should hope so," grinned Danny. "After all, it is supposed to be a notice!"

The two girls pulled faces and pretended to groan. But Anna smiled at Danny – that was the first joke she'd heard him crack. Maybe the Millington puppies were already helping him to "get sorted out"?

As soon as they pinned the notice on the board in the entrance hall, Anna was flooded with enquiries.

"How old are they?"

"What breed?"

"I'll have those three!" This last was from a little boy in class one who pointed to the ones he liked best.

"You'll have to ask your mum and dad," Anna told him. "And I don't think they'd want three puppies all at the same time."

"Oh, they don't want any puppies," he said. "I'll keep them in the shed with my guinea-pigs and rabbits. I've got a spare hutch."

Anna shook her head. "You can't keep puppies in cages," she said. "They grow too big – and anyway, they need company."

"But I want some for my collection," said the boy.

"Not puppies, you don't," said Anna. "Try hamsters."

Other people came up and asked about the dogs, but Anna always referred them to the phone number.

"You have to get your parents to ring," she explained. "The puppies can only go to good homes."

And most of the children gave up, knowing their parents would never agree. Many already had dogs or other pets, some lived on farms where only working dogs were allowed, others in small cottages with no room for pets indoors. Still, one or two parents did ring Mrs Bright, enquiring after the pups, so she was pleased about the notice.

"What's all this they're telling me about the lovely little puppies on the poster?" she asked. "I didn't give you any pictures."

"The new boy, Danny Forester, drew them," Anna said. "And they do look so sweet…"

"But how did he know what they looked like?" asked her mother.

"Oh, I just described them — I mean, the drawings aren't absolutely accurate, but they are the right sort of colour and breed."

"Whatever that is," smiled her mother.

"If Danny Forester's mum rings to enquire, try to persuade her they need a puppy," Anna told her. "He wants one really badly and she won't agree."

"What about his dad?" asked Mrs Bright.

And suddenly Anna realized she knew nothing about a Mr Forester. She shrugged.

"Don't know," she said. "But I get the feeling his mum's in charge."

"In which case, unless she changes her mind, I wouldn't dream of letting the boy have a pup."

"But maybe if she speaks to you…"

Mrs Bright shook her head. "You know my rule, Anna," she said. "If in doubt say no!"

Anna sighed. She knew her mother was right: anybody who wasn't absolutely sure about owning a dog shouldn't get one. And if the Foresters were still settling themselves in they wouldn't want a little pup around. On the other hand, six weeks was a long time —

maybe by then Danny's mum would weaken.

But Danny's mother never even rang to enquire about the pups. Anna thought how lonely Danny must be – a pup would make a great companion for him. Danny himself seemed to have given up any idea of having a dog – he'd never mentioned the pups since the day he made the poster.

Then, one day he surprised her. Amy was away with earache so Anna walked to the bus on her own. Suddenly she felt a tug at her shoulder. She turned round and saw Danny, tagging alongside.

"These pups of yours…" he said. "Are they farm dogs? Mum said working dogs need a job to do or they're a nuisance."

"She's right," Anna said. "But I don't think ours are working dogs. The mother wouldn't have been allowed to stray if she'd been a useful farm dog."

"What about the father?"

Anna shrugged. "Nobody knows," she said. "Looking at that all-over black one he could have been a labrador, but the others are more of a mixture."

"Can I come to see them?" said Danny.

"Of course, but they're a bit small just now – why don't you come over in the holidays?" she suggested. "They'll be old enough to handle then."

"I'll be away," he said, gloomily.

"On holiday?" asked Anna brightly. "Lucky you!" Apart from trips with Amy or visits to her Grandma in Cornwall, Anna had never been away on holiday – her parents were always too busy on the farm.

"I'm going to my dad's," Danny replied, gruffly.

Something in his voice made Anna hesitate before she said anything more. So Danny's dad wasn't living in Millington then – that was why she'd only ever seen his mother. "Does he live far away?" she asked, casually.

"Near London," he said.

"Oh, lucky you – spending your holidays in London!" Anna said, brightly. "I've never been to London."

Danny shrugged and turned away. "No, but you do live with your mum and your dad," he said, in a choked voice.

Anna suddenly felt embarrassed. "Look," she said, hastily. "I'll ask my mum if you can come over and see the pups before you go away."

"Would you?" Danny brightened up. "You see, I thought if I could just see them, I could tell Dad all about them…" His voice faded.

"Well, we could always save one for you," said Anna. "They won't be ready to leave until next term."

"Wouldn't that be great!" Danny smiled. But then his face dropped. "It's no use – I don't suppose Mum would ever agree." He looked down the road to where his mother had parked her little maroon and cream 2CV. "She says she's got enough to do, setting up the pottery."

"Pottery? You mean you live over at Potter's Cott?"

He nodded. "Do you know it?" he asked.

"I don't know it," Anna replied. "But I can see it, from our attic window. You live straight across the valley from me."

"Perhaps you could hold up each one of the puppies in turn for me to see," grinned Danny.

"Don't be daft – you just come over and see for yourself," said Anna, jumping on to the bus step. "There's a footpath down to the river, over the bridge then right up to our farm – you can walk all the way."

"On my own?" asked Danny, who was used to city streets but not quiet country paths.

"Bring your mother – she'll never be able to resist our puppies!"

"Don't you believe it!" Danny waved and ran off down the road.

Anna watched his mother getting out of the car to call him. Mrs Forester had a mass of fuzzy black hair and a sharp white face which looked quite fierce just then. She smiled to greet Danny, but it was what Anna's dad called a "mouth-only smile" – her eyes peered under her fringe, sharp with anxiety.

Anna thought about the Forester family all the way home. Why had Danny's mother moved out of town? she wondered. And why did she look so unhappy?

She'd be happier with a puppy to keep her company while Danny's at school, Anna thought. It was her opinion that everyone would be happier with a puppy for company – especially Anna Bright! Anna had a sudden vision of little Runty, still crawling up too late for meals, still being pushed around by the other fat, thriving pups.

"He'd be very happy with a nice, quiet owner like Danny," she told herself. But she suddenly realized she wouldn't be at all happy to let him go – to Danny or to anyone else. Runty was her own special pup – no matter what Dad said about not getting attached to the strays. After all, Runty wasn't really a stray – he was born and reared at Millington Farm, along with his five brothers and sisters. And surely, even Dad couldn't resist a gentle little puppy like Runty?

Chapter 3

When Anna told Danny he could come and see the pups before he went away, he merely shrugged and looked so gloomy that she quickly dropped the subject.

But their notice had aroused a lot of interest and several people came to see the puppies once they were old enough to be disturbed, though nobody had offered them a home yet.

Then one Saturday morning Anna heard a great commotion outside the kitchen door as a vehicle swept into the yard and skidded to a halt. Rufus barked excitedly and even before Anna could get out to call him in, she became aware of several different barks, hectic now and from all directions. She rushed out to see

three dogs tearing madly around the yard —
Rufus and two huge black labradors, who had
obviously just jumped out of the shining black
Range Rover which was parked by the stables.

"Rufus – stop that!" Anna called. She knew
her mother was very particular about Rufus
playing with other people's dogs; some
owners didn't like it and some of their dogs
could be quite nasty. "Rufus – here boy!" she
called again.

But when Rufus arrived at the kitchen door,
he brought the two labradors with him.
Grinning wildly, they hurled themselves at
Anna.

"Hey!" she exclaimed. "Get down – down!"

The dogs had obviously never obeyed an
order in their little lives; pushing Anna aside,
they raced into the kitchen, pausing only to
gollup the remains of Rufus's breakfast before
setting up a race-track round and round the
kitchen table.

"Stop! Stop!" cried Anna. "Rufus – SIT!"

But even the biddable Rufus was too hyped
up to take notice. Anna turned to the man
standing by the Range Rover.

"Could you call your dogs out, please?" she asked.

The man laughed. "If you keep yours in," he said. "I thought this was a dog sanctuary, not a circus!"

Anna gritted her teeth. She didn't think much of his joke but she knew she couldn't answer back. "I'll keep Rufus in here," she said.

The man gave a sharp whistle. "Harvey! Henry! Here, boys!" he called.

But the "boys" went on with their race around the kitchen without apparently even hearing their master's call. Tongues lolling, mouths grinning, tails sweeping the cutlery from the table, they had no intention of giving up such a good game.

Anna watched in dismay. If only she could catch Rufus, maybe he'd calm them all down. She waited for him to pass, grabbed his collar and pushed his hindquarters down.

"Sit!" she hissed in his ear. And although he whined and stretched his neck towards the others, he did as he was told.

Suddenly there came a loud and piercing

whistle which Anna felt, rather than heard, in her ears. Startled, Rufus jumped, then dropped, trembling, to the ground, quite upset by the sound.

"Here, boys – do as you're told, damn you!"

The man from the Range Rover dropped his dog-whistle where it dangled on a cord around his neck. He strode into the kitchen, grabbed his two dogs by their choke-chain collars and dragged them out to the yard.

"Shut that animal inside," he yelled to Anna as he passed. "Then I might be able to get mine to calm down."

I doubt it, thought Anna, who resented Rufus being called "that animal". Nevertheless, she shut the door firmly behind her and went across the yard. The man had clipped chains on his dogs now, and they stood choking and straining by the car.

"Where's your father?" he asked.

"Dad?" Anna was surprised. "He's out on the fields. Did you want to see him?"

"I want to see these pups you're advertising."

"Oh – it's Mum you need to talk to. She does the dogs, Dad does the farm," Anna explained. And she noticed that there were passengers in the car: a woman and a girl, both with short blonde hair, beautifully shaped in an expensively simple style. Anna smiled up at them. Neither of them smiled back.

"I'll ring the bell for Mum," she said to the man. "She's up with the dogs right now."

"Oh, don't worry, just show me the way and I'll go and find her," he said, hauling the two great dogs back to heel.

"No, you can't do that," said Anna, more sharply than she'd meant to.

"Oh, and why not, young lady?" he asked.

"You can't take your dogs into the stables," Anna explained. She was about to say they might spread diseases, but something about the man's attitude warned her to be tactful. "They might catch something," she said.

"You mean your dogs are diseased?" he asked, turning puce.

"No – they've all been vaccinated, but some of the strays are new to us. The vaccine takes a day or two to work."

The man snorted. "We don't want any second-rate sickly pups," he said.

The woman passenger let the window down and leaned out.

"Oh, do come on, Charles," she said. "It's very boring sitting here."

"Then get yourself down here, my darling," he replied, not at all fondly. "And get that girl out – she's the one who's choosing."

Choosing? Anna felt a sudden spasm of panic – these people sounded quite serious.

"I'm not sure..." she began.

But at that moment, to her relief, her mother appeared round the corner of the stables. She was wearing her usual jeans and muddy wellies, with one of Dad's old sweaters hanging almost to her knees.

In contrast, the Range Rover ladies were clad in immaculate green Barbours and shining green boots, unspecked by country dirt. How did they keep them so clean, Anna wondered; after the past week's rain the countryside was sodden and mud-soaked and nobody in Millington wore clean boots.

"Good morning!" Her mother came forward to greet the party. She moved along- side the man and just touched the choking labradors lightly on their necks. "Hello, boys," she said, softly. "Sit, then – good fellows."

And, to the man's obvious amazement, they sat, gazing adoringly up at Mrs Bright, who rubbed their shoulders and murmured approvingly.

"We've come about a couple of pups," the man said abruptly.

"Oh, yes?" Mrs Bright waited.

"Yes – for Lisa-Jayne, my daughter." He stood back and nudged the girl forward. She stood gazing straight ahead without actually looking at anyone.

"Hello, Lisa-Jayne," said Mrs Bright. "This is my daughter, Anna."

"Hello," said Anna, more cheerfully than she felt.

Lisa-Jayne merely nodded.

"Well, then, we'd better get on, Mrs … er…" said the man.

"Bright – Laura Bright," smiled Anna's mother. She held out a rather dirty hand.

"Lennox-Browne," said the man, ignoring the hand. "My wife." He nodded in the direction of the blonde woman, who, just like her daughter, nodded to thin air. "Now then, just take us to see the pups," he went on, yanking the labradors to their feet by the choke-chains.

Anna saw her mother wince: she didn't approve of chains.

"Not with your dogs," she said, firmly. "They'll upset the pups' mother."

Mr Lennox-Browne looked as if he was going to argue the point, but Laura Bright looked steadily at him and he seemed to get her message.

"Right – you can hold these," he said, addressing his wife. "Lisa-Jayne can come and choose her puppies."

"And as soon as you disappear these two will want to chase after you," Mrs Lennox-Browne pointed out. "They'll pull so hard they'll have me over. Put them back in the car."

They glared at each other and the dogs began to whine.

"If Lisa-Jayne is the one looking for a puppy, why not let Anna take her up to see the litter?" suggested Mrs Bright. "I don't like too many people up there – the pups are only a few weeks old, you know."

"Right – off you go then, Lisa-Jayne. The little girl will show you the way. I'll have a talk with Laura here, check the pups out..." Mr Lennox-Browne smiled broadly at Mrs Bright.

Anna glared at him. Who did he think he was, calling her "the little girl" and her mother "Laura"? But she caught a warning glance from her mother and turned to smile stiffly at Lisa-Jayne.

"Come on, then," she said. "I'll show you the way."

Lisa-Jayne Lennox-Browne, what a name, thought Anna as they walked together in silence up to the stables. She must write her name with two hyphens! Anna glanced at the elegant figure at her side. Lisa-Jayne was taller than her and with her sophisticated hair-cut and her pearly varnished nails, she looked a lot older – a teenager, really. Surely she'd be too busy with exams and homework – not to mention parties and boyfriends – to have time for two puppies?

Of course, she might just be dog-crazy like herself, but somehow she didn't look it – she'd totally ignored her father's labradors.

"Here we are," Anna said, scrambling up the half-door to reach the bolt. "Come on in. I'll have to bolt the door again, just in case."

She led the girl to the stable where the pups lived. Their mother was having a rest in a separate stall so they were squiggling and squealing all round their big plastic bed.

The two girls stood leaning over the short door, watching the pups.

"There are three males and three females," Anna explained. "I'm afraid I can't tell you which is which from here but by next week we'll be able to pick them up without up-setting their mother." She smiled fondly down at the wriggling mass of bodies. "Aren't they sweet!" she murmured. "Look at that one over there – that's Joey; he's so funny, like a clown, with his black patch over one eye and that grin, and there's Runty – the littlest one, bless him – he nearly didn't survive, you know…"

Anna stopped chattering, partly because she suddenly realized she might arouse too much interest in her beloved Runty, but also because she'd caught sight of the girl's expression. Most people would turn quite soft and dewy-eyed at the sight of the puppies playing together; even Anna, who saw them several times a day, could hardly drag herself away from them. But Lisa-Jayne's face was quite blank and she glared stolidly at the opposite wall.

"What kind do you want?" Anna asked, softly.

"What do you mean?" Lisa-Jayne asked.

"I mean male or female? All black, part white, or a bit patchy? Brave and bold or sweet and shy? They all have different personalities, you know."

"You like dogs, don't you?" Lisa-Jayne broke in, suddenly.

Anna looked at her in amazement.

"Like dogs?" she asked, thinking the girl might as well have asked if she liked breathing or eating. "Well, of course I like dogs." She paused, light suddenly dawning. "Don't you?" she asked.

Lisa-Jayne slowly shook her head. Her

shiny, bobbed hair swung across her face, hiding it from Anna's view.

"They're disgusting!" she said, looking down into the sodden newspaper that lined the puppies' den.

"Oh – only for a few weeks," Anna reassured her. "They're soon house-trained."

"To do all their messes in the garden," said Lisa-Jayne. "And to chew your best pair of shoes, tear up your handbag, eat your French homework..." She sounded close to tears.

"Is that what Harvey and Henry have done?" asked Anna, suppressing a giggle.

Lisa-Jayne nodded mournfully. "It's all Dad's fault," she said. "He's always wanted to live in the country, big house, paddock, horses, dogs – real country gentleman, you know?"

Anna didn't. Everyone she knew lived in tiny cottages or on sprawling farms, working all hours in all weathers to scrape a living from the land. Definitely not "country gentlemen" – even the women spent most of their time in oily overalls, ancient waxed jackets and anoraks, up to their knees in mud and worse.

"He won the lottery, you know," said Lisa-Jayne, tucking her beautiful hair behind an ear in which a jewel sparkled – a diamond? Anna wondered, after digesting this last piece of news.

"He sold up his garage business, and our house, and moved us out here, away from everybody," Lisa-Jayne went on. She didn't seem to mind talking to a "little girl", thought Anna. It was almost as if she was talking to herself.

"And I go to a new school – private, all girls, where we wear horrible tartan kilts and woolly cardigans and everybody's mad on horses." She gave a deep, shuddering sigh and looked down into the stable once more. "I don't want a puppy," she broke out. "I want my friends back home and the shops and the cinemas and the discos…"

She sniffed loudly then pulled a brand-new handkerchief from her Barbour pocket and delicately blew her nose.

"Why don't you tell your dad?" Anna asked her.

"I can't tell *him* anything," said Lisa-Jayne.

"Not even my own name – Lisa Lennox – that's what it was before…" She broke off and, for the first time, looked anxiously into Anna's face. "You won't tell him I told you – about the lottery, I mean?"

"Of course not!" Anna was indignant. She wouldn't tell that man anything if she could help it. She thought for a moment, intrigued by the idea that anyone so rich could be so unhappy. "Look, Mum could say you've got enough on with those naughty labradors without taking any more puppies," she said. "I mean, that's true really."

"He won't listen," said Lisa-Jayne, miserably.

"He will to my mum!" said Anna. "It wouldn't surprise me if he isn't listening to her right now. Come on!"

This time, Lisa-Jayne bolted the half-door and they ran down the path to the farmyard together.

"Look!" Anna pulled back before they got on to the cobbles and nodded across the farmyard. "Told you!"

Laura Bright was leading two docile black

labradors round the yard, pausing occasionally to tell them to sit. They sat.

"How does she do that?" asked Lisa-Jayne in amazement.

"Bribery and corruption," laughed Anna. "Just watch her hands."

As she spoke, her mother held up both hands, tightly clenched, and said something to the dogs, who immediately went flat down at her feet. Mrs Bright then held out a biscuit to each dog. The sound of crunching could be heard even at that distance.

"Do anything for food, labradors," said Anna.

"Including stopping knocking me over?" asked Lisa-Jayne.

"If you've got enough biscuits," Anna grinned. "Ask Mum for some training tips."

But when they joined the others they found they were too late for that.

"Well, Mrs Bright, I'm very impressed," Mr Lennox-Browne was saying. "If you could give these two a bit of training, whilst we're in Kenya, it would be a great relief."

"I could do that," said Mrs Bright, thoughtfully. "But it won't work unless I give you some training, too.

"You're on!" said Mr Lennox-Browne. "When can you start?"

"Oh, I've already started," Mrs Bright assured him. "But we'll need some regular sessions..." She broke off as the two girls approached. "Hello, girls, were the pups all right?"

"They're fine, Mum," said Anna, pulling a face and frantically trying to send complicated signals to her mother.

But Lisa-Jayne smiled at Mrs Bright. "Are you going to train the new puppies along with Harvey and Henry?" she asked, sweetly.

Mrs Bright shook her head. "Oh no, they're far too young." She turned to the other couple. "You know, I think you'll be quite busy enough getting these two knocked into shape without starting on another pair just now."

From the car, Mrs Lennox-Browne nodded her sleek blonde head. "She's right, Chas," she said. "Let's get Harvey and Henry under control, have our holiday, and think about a pet for Lisa when we get back."

"I wish you two would make your minds up," said Mr Lennox-Browne.

"We have," said his wife. "Leave the puppies and let's get back to Winterspit."

"Is that where you live?" asked Mrs Bright.

"That's where we live!" agreed Mr Lennox-Browne, with some pride. "You must come over with your mother some time. There's a lovely pool…"

Anna was impressed. Winterspit Hall was not only an old manor house, it had once been the home of some famous rock star or other and she'd built tennis courts, a swimming-pool, stabling for her valuable horses – which she never rode – and even her own cinema in the old ballroom. Winterspit was a legend in Millington and very few people had ever been there.

"Thank you," said Anna. Lisa-Jayne was just thoroughly miserable, she thought: her father was really quite a kind-hearted man!

"Kind-hearted, wrong-headed," said her dad

when she told him all about the Lennox-Brownes' visit later that day. "That poor girl needs a friend, not a dog."

"That poor girl is probably extremely wealthy," said Laura Bright. "I mean, if they've bought Winterspit Hall they must be seriously rich."

Anna said nothing.

"One thing's for certain," her mother went on. "I'll charge them a good rate for the training sessions – make up for not selling a pup to them."

"Does that mean we could afford to keep one of the pups?" asked Anna, innocently.

"Now then, Anna," said her dad. "How often have I told you not to get attached to one special pup?"

"Oh, I'm not, Dad!" Anna assured him. "I'm attached to them all!"

Which was true, she told herself, though she had to admit it was little Runty who'd stolen her heart!

Chapter 4

On the last day of term, Anna decided she'd have to pluck up courage and speak to Danny Forester about the pups.

"I know he's dying to see them," she told Amy. "And if he doesn't come now they'll all be spoken for before he gets back from his holiday."

"But what if his mum won't let him have one?" asked Amy.

"We'll have to think of a way of persuading her," said Anna. "Danny's so shy and lonely up there at Potter's Cott – I'm sure he needs a pup."

"So do I, but that doesn't persuade *my* mum," said Amy, mournfully.

"But you've got lots of friends and your gran's lovely cats. And you spend half your time with our animals – you're not like Danny."

"Poor little Danny," agreed Amy. "Hey – perhaps he'd like that poor little pup." Amy had been to see the pups several times now, and she was already good at telling them apart.

"Which one?" asked Anna.

"You know – the one you told me about, that was born later. The one who's always pushed around by the others."

Anna looked at her thoughtfully. "Why him?" she asked.

"Well, they're a bit alike, aren't they? I mean, smaller than the others, nobody to play with, a bit on their own…"

"That doesn't mean to say Danny would want a puppy like himself," said Anna, sharply. She couldn't help feeling that Runty belonged to her – after all, he might have died if she hadn't spotted him being born!

Nevertheless, she felt she had to mention the puppies again to Danny, who was looking paler and more miserable than usual just then.

"I hope you have a good time in London," she said, by way of starting a conversation. "It must be great to see all the famous places, the shops, cinemas, museums…"

"Been there, done that," said Danny, gloomily.

"What, everything in the whole of London?" asked Anna, in disbelief.

"Everything we can afford," he said. "It costs us nearly ten pounds just to get into London itself – we'll probably only go up for a day."

"So what will you do the rest of the time?"

Danny brightened. "Oh, go for walks along the river, and biking in Richmond Park – a huge wild park near where Dad lives."

"So he lives near some open country, then," said Anna, thoughtfully.

"Oh yes – but not with farms and animals like round here." Danny was about to turn away, but he paused and asked, "Have you ever been to the wilds of Surrey?"

"No," Anna grinned. "We've got quite

enough wilds up at our farm." She took a deep breath and pressed on. "Why don't you come over and look round before you go away?"

Danny stared at her, long and hard. "Do you mean that?" he asked.

"Of course I do," she assured him. "There's the sheep and the lambs and a few bullocks out to grass just now…"

"And what about those puppies?" he asked, eagerly.

"Oh yes – you can see all of those now, they're quite old enough." Anna kept her voice casual but she could see the glimmer of excitement in Danny's eyes.

He sighed. "I'll ask Mum," he said. "But she's so busy setting up the pottery…"

"Well, there's the bridle-path straight down the valley to our place. It's a bit muddy just now, but an easy walk – you don't need a lift, just come on your own."

Danny looked at her in amazement. "Mum would never send me off on my own," he said.

"Why not?"

"It's dangerous."

"Not on the bridle-path – nobody would let a bull loose just there."

"I wasn't thinking of bulls," said Danny.

"So what were you thinking of?"

He paused, deep in thought.

"In town there's always the traffic, Saturdays there's football crowds, and sometimes a bit of aggro in the streets – Mum would never let me out alone…"

"Tell her the most danger you'd ever meet on the bridle-path is the hunt – and it's not the season."

"I don't think I'll mention the hunt to my mum," grinned Danny. "Look – I'll get a lift over and walk back – you can point out the way."

"Right!" said Anna, delighted at her success. "See you tomorrow."

"What time?"

"Time?" Anna thought for a moment. Time didn't matter in the holidays, she'd be at home all day. "Any time," she said.

"'First catch your hare'," said Amy, when

Anna told her the news as the school bus trundled them along the deep Devon lanes that afternoon.

"What does that mean?" asked Anna. "We're talking about pups, not hares."

"My dad's always saying that. It's a quote from some famous cookery book – I think he means get the hardest bit over first before you go any further."

"Oh, I don't think getting Danny over to Millington Sanctuary is the hardest bit."

"No," agreed Amy. "There's still his mum…"

"And his dad," said Anna, thoughtfully. "You know he doesn't live in the centre of London at all. He's near a big wild park, and the river."

"So you think *he'll* let Danny have a puppy?"

Anna shrugged. "I don't know," she admitted. "But if Danny sees one he likes and he's really keen, he might try to persuade him this holidays."

"But what would happen to the puppy when he comes back here?"

"I expect the puppy would want to come with him," smiled Anna. "And who could resist a puppy's pleading look?"

"Danny's mum, perhaps?" suggested Amy.

The very next day, Anna found someone who resisted all the puppies' pleading looks.

She woke bright and early, as she always did on holiday and weekends, and this – glory be – was both! She pulled on her sweatshirt and jeans and ran downstairs to the kitchen.

"Scrambled eggs or rice pudding?" she asked her mother.

"For breakfast?" asked Dad.

"For puppies' breakfasts," she said.

The pups were being weaned now, eating some of the foods they would be given when they left their mother.

"Open a tin of rice," said Mrs Bright. "I haven't collected the eggs yet. Perhaps you and Amy could do that later?"

"Of course," Anna agreed. "And there's somebody else coming from school – Danny Forester from over at Potter's Cott."

"Oh – the newcomers? That was kind of

you to ask him over," said her mother. "Still wants a dog, does he?"

"Danny does, his mother doesn't," said Anna tersely.

"I see!" said Dad. "Is this one of your puppy plots, Anna?"

"Not exactly," said Anna, smiling. "But Danny's lonely up there and do you know, his mum won't let him out on his own – not ever."

Mr and Mrs Bright exchanged glances.

"Well, if they've just moved in that's probably the right thing to do," said Dad. "New folk can get lost in these lanes, you know."

"When he's seen all he wants round here you could show him the bridle-path back to Potter's," suggested Mum. "Help him find his way around. But first – feed those pups, clean out the stable, and get the eggs – in that order…"

Anna loved feeding the pups. Their mother was taken off to her private stable for her own feed, then the newspapers were cleared from the floor and fresh ones put in, and finally a big bowl of rice pudding was put down and the pups pushed and shoved to get their little noses into it.

Except for Runty, who hung back, shivering, obviously hoping there'd be something left when the others moved away.

"Come on, Runty – get stuck in!" said Anna.

Lifting the little dog over the squirming bodies she pushed a couple of pups aside and put Runty down at the edge of the bowl. Soon, his little white muzzle was thrust into the pudding and he slurped away along with the others.

He was getting a bit more confidence, thought Anna, though he still needed a bit of a push to get him going. Like Danny, she suddenly thought, feeling quite excited at the idea of showing him round that morning. But glad, all the same, that Amy would be here, too. She wasn't shy of anyone.

Now the dish was empty, except for the pup Anna called Joey the Clown, who was skidding about on it like a comic ice-skater. The rest of the puppies had scattered now, some back to bed, others to scramble and fight all over the floor. Anna had just picked up the dish and was about to sneak out of the half-door when the yard bell rang.

That'll be Amy, she thought. But surely Amy would go into the kitchen or come straight up here? She knew the farm as well as Anna did. Maybe it was Danny then? Anna bolted the outer door and ran down to the yard eagerly.

But it was neither. Beside a Volvo estate car an elderly couple were talking to Mrs Bright.

"...can't face taking on another pup," the woman was saying. "And it wouldn't be fair — we're getting on now."

"Speak for yourself, old lady!" said her husband. "I'll take on any pup..."

"No you won't — it'll be me who has to clean up after it, house-train it, mop it up and bath it. You just do all the fun bits — walkies and feeds," smiled the woman. "No, I think something a little older would be better."

"Come on up and see our older dogs," said Mrs Bright. "Anna — can you take Mr and

Mrs Neill along to the stables while I finish off feeding the geese?" She turned to the couple. "Anna is my daughter – she knows all the dogs. I'll join you in a minute…"

Anna led the couple into the stables where four stray dogs were living, as well as the bitch and her pups.

"How long has he been here?" asked Mr Neill, looking over the half-door at a burly brown boxer-cross.

"Ten days," said Anna, who kept count of all the dogs' arrivals. "Bruno's very gentle, not a stray – his owners have gone abroad."

"He's a fine specimen," said Mr Neill.

Catching the admiring tone in his voice, Bruno came over, stood up on his hind legs and plonked his jowls over the door. Mr Neill cautiously patted his huge head and Bruno began to slobber.

"There's a grand fellow," said Mr Neill, surreptitiously wiping his slobbery hands on his trousers.

"There's a messy dog," said his wife, watching him closely. "And he's too big for our little bungalow."

They moved from pen to pen, discussing the dogs – and dismissing them one by one. This was too hairy, that too small, another too yappy… Anna began to suspect that they didn't really want a dog at all. She was about to show them the way out when Mrs Neill peered over the last pen and exclaimed,

"Oh, aren't you a lovely – look here, Joe, she's a beauty – spitting image of our old Jill!"

It was the mother of the pups, taking a rest while she had a chance.

"Oh but…" Anna stopped. Was the bitch for sale? After all there was no need for them to keep her, once the pups were weaned.

"Anything wrong with her?" asked Mr Neill.

"Oh no – she's a lovely, gentle dog," said Anna. "Only she's feeding pups just now."

"When will she stop?"

"When the pups have gone, I suppose," said Anna.

"How many did she have?"

"Six – three males, three females." Anna almost chanted the reply, she'd said it so often now.

"And how many have gone?"

"Well, none yet," Anna admitted. "They're only a few weeks old."

Mrs Bright clattered through the outer door. "Everything all right?" she asked, cheerfully. "Have you found your own special dog?" Mrs Bright believed in dogs like other people believed in marriage – there was a doggy Mr Right out there just meant for you sometime…

"Yes, I think we have," said Mrs Neill, smiling fondly down at the little bitch. "We'll call her Jilly – after our last collie."

"Come on in and meet her before you decide," said Mrs Bright.

She unbolted the door and led "Jilly" out of the pen. Mr Neill bent down to examine her teeth and he picked up her paws one at a time.

"She's in fine fettle," he told his wife.

"Of course she is," she said. "Look at those bright eyes and that tail – look at her lovely coat!"

They patted and exclaimed over the little cross-collie, who responded by rubbing herself against their legs and wagging her tail furiously.

And so it was settled. Jilly was to go to the Neills just as soon as all the pups were weaned. Meantime, they would come back and visit her regularly, take her for walks, and get to know her.

"Well, we don't seem to be selling any pups," sighed Mrs Bright, as she and Anna waved the Neills off. "So far, I've got one training job, and sold one adult dog, but that still leaves us with six pups!"

"And they're all squealing for their mother now," smiled Anna, peering over their door.

"Come on, then, Jilly – back on duty," said Mrs Bright. "We must use her new name all the time now," she told Anna. "And speed up the weaning process if she's ever to get free of those greedy pups."

"Good girl, Jilly," Anna told the bitch, as she settled herself down amongst the wriggling puppies. "Make sure Runty gets a drink!"

Down in the yard the stable bell began to ring.

"Maybe this time we'll sell a pup," said Mum hopefully.

But when Anna saw who it was, she wasn't so sure.

Chapter 5

It was a little maroon and cream Citroën – the kind with a cloth top that you can roll back in hot weather. Danny stood by it, looking small and embarrassed, whilst his mother pulled fiercely on the bell-rope at the corner of the outhouse.

"Coming!" called Mrs Bright, dashing down the path from the stables.

Anna followed slowly, watching Danny's mother pacing the yard impatiently, her pale face scrunched up in a frown. Not much chance of tempting her with a puppy just now, she decided.

And by the time she arrived in the yard, Danny's mum was getting back into the car.

"Don't worry – we'll see him home," Mrs Bright was saying.

"I don't want him wandering around on his own," warned Danny's mother.

"No – of course not. AnnarandAmy will bring him. They know the way – been walking up there since they were small."

"And you let them?" asked Mrs Forester, quite shocked.

"Only as far as the top stile, where we can keep an eye on them. But as they're with Danny they can go as far as your cottage – if you could just walk them back along the ridge..."

"I'll do that," Mrs Forester agreed. "Right – lunch at one, Danny. Don't be late or I'll be worried."

Danny merely nodded and went on looking at his shoes.

Just then, Amy's dad drove into the yard, leaving just enough room for the Citroën to get past. With a flurry of gravel, Mrs Forester swept off down the lane.

"Hey, Danny, glad you could come over! Am I in time for the eggs, Anna?" Amy scrambled out of the car, already chatting happily, and the atmosphere suddenly lightened. Whilst Mrs Bright and Amy's dad exchanged news, the three children set off with the egg basket up the field to the hen-runs.

It was the start of a very happy morning. Danny seemed to come alive on the farm, as he never did in school. He wiped the eggs while Amy sorted them into sizes and Anna packed them into half-dozen boxes. And all the time he was chatting happily, asking questions about the animals and the farm.

He hadn't mentioned the pups, Anna noticed. She wondered if he was saving them until last, like she saved the black fruit pastilles until all the boring orange and lemon ones had gone.

Amy never saved anything until last – she just took whatever came her way. "Now, what about those gorgeous pups?" she asked, when they'd finished the eggs.

"Those gorgeous pups are full of breakfast and fast asleep," said Anna. "I thought we'd walk up to see the bullocks first."

"Oh, yes – you must see the sweet little bullocks, Danny," said Amy.

Danny looked doubtful. "Can even a little bull be sweet?" he asked.

"He can at Millington Farm," Amy laughed.

They walked down the track to the meadow, where the two girls clambered on to the gate. As soon as they were settled, the bullocks gathered around them, full of curiosity. The girls scratched their hard, curly heads, which, Danny was relieved to see, had no horns. He pushed a cautious hand through the railings and touched one of the animals. It turned its head and stared at him with huge, mild eyes.

"Go on – stroke his nose," Amy said.

Gently, Danny stroked the beast's damp nose. The bullock lifted its head and nudged Danny's hand, wanting him to go on.

"He's tame!" Danny exclaimed.

"Well, they're not wild buffalo!" laughed Amy.

"They were when they first arrived," said Anna. "They used to scatter about all over the place. But now they've got used to us they're quite calm and confident." She ruffled the golden curls on the top of the nearest bullock's head.

"Confident – yeah, that's right," Danny murmured into the nearest bullock's ear. And Anna got the impression he was talking more

to himself than to the animal.

"So when can we see the pups?" Amy asked again.

"Oh, come on, then," said Anna. "They'll have had their morning nap and Jilly will be wanting a break..."

"Jilly?" asked Amy. "Who's she?"

"Their mother," grinned Anna. "We've found a home for her – and a name."

They raced down from the meadows to the stables, where Amy and Danny waited while Anna went down to ask her mother if they could go in to the pups.

"Can't find her," she said, when she returned. "Must have gone down the long field to Dad. Still – I often sort out the pups on my own – come on!"

The puppies were old enough to come out and wander around in the stables now; squeaking and squealing they rolled and scrambled out of their stall like a moving jelly. Anna shut them out of the stall so that Jilly could have a rest and Amy chased them wildly around the stable.

Danny stood quite still, watching the pups

wriggling and widdling all over his trainers, afraid to move in case he trod on one.

"Shoo, you lot!" Anna said, advancing on the pups unceremoniously. "Come on – we'll take you out the back."

She and Amy shepherded the pups along to the back door, which opened out on to a little yard. Drawn by the bright light, the puppies bounded out and immediately fell to chasing and biting and clambering on top of each other, squealing and squeaking like little piglets. Amy ran after them, catching first one, then another, and laughing all the time, while Danny crouched by the wall at the end of the yard, obviously fascinated by the little creatures.

Runty staggered out into the yard last of all. He tried to crawl up Anna's wellingtons, leaving wet puddles behind him.

"Come on, then, little Runty," said Anna, softly. She picked him up and snuggled him on to her shoulder. His breath smelt smoky and warm on her face and his little black ears felt like satin in her fingers.

"Oh – I've got that freckly face one!" said

Amy, holding the pup up to her own freckly face. "Isn't she cute?"

The cute, freckly pup reached out for something to nibble and found Amy's chin.

"Ow!" she laughed, almost dropping her. "Their teeth are sharp as needles!"

"Yes, we're feeding them a few puppy nuts each day now, ready for when they leave us."

"Have you sold any?" asked Danny, who was still crouched by the wall, observing the pups rather than handling them.

"No," said Anna. "Only the mother."

She looked at Danny closely, trying to guess what he was thinking. Was he longing to take one of the pups? Was he working out how to ask his mum? But Danny was his usual silent self, except that he was smiling happily at the antics of three pups in the corner of the yard.

"I think we ought to take them back, now," said Anna, suddenly remembering she hadn't checked with Mum about letting them out.

"Come on, you lot, let's be having you!" called Amy. But the little pups scuttled away and rolled in a heap, obviously enjoying the chasing game.

Laughing and coaxing, they finally managed to get the pups penned up. Jilly wagged her tail in welcome as they surged up her and started to drink. AnnarandAmy wandered off to look at the strays on the other side of the stables but Danny couldn't take his eyes off the puppies.

"Thought you said there were six?" he said, suddenly.

"Yes, that's right," said Anna, adding automatically, "three males, three females."

"No there's not," Danny told her. "One, two, three, four — and that one at the end — five."

"Are you sure?" Anna ran back and peered over the old gate.

"Maybe that runty one is hiding in the straw," suggested Amy.

"No — he's the one at the end, look!" Danny pointed to the littlest puppy, sucking blissfully on the end teat, all by himself.

"Oh my goodness!" said Anna. "We've left one outside."

"No we haven't," said Amy. "I had a good look round before I shut the door."

"Which one is missing?" Danny asked,

peering at the animals, all flat out and sucking greedily.

"Well, I brought Runty and the jet black bitch." Anna pointed at the two pups.

"And I had the freckle-face and black-hat over there," said Amy.

"That's one dog and three bitches..." Anna was trying desperately to sort them all out. "That leaves..."

"Two dogs," said Danny. "And I caught the one with a stripe down his face like a badger."

"Badger – good name for him," said Amy. "So which one's missing?"

"Joey the Clown," Anna groaned. "I might have known."

"Why?"

"Oh, he's never frightened of anything – he can nearly climb out of the stall now, and he's always up to some trick or other – swimming in the milk, rolling in the feed-bowl... Now where's he got to?"

"I know the one you mean," said Amy. "But I didn't see him in the yard."

"No," agreed Danny. "I had three in my corner, you were busy with the freckly one, and Anna had the runty one – that only makes five. I reckon he never came out with us."

"So where did he go?" asked Anna, fighting back panic. "He wasn't outside and he's not in the pen…"

"He must be in between," said Danny, calmly. "In the stables, here."

They walked up and down the alley between the rows of stalls, peering all round for any sign of a little fat pup.

"Joey – here, boy!" called Amy, until Anna pointed out that the pup didn't know his name.

"Oh, where can he be?" asked Anna, quite tearful now. She was getting desperate – a four-week puppy out on his own could be in all kinds of danger. And what would her mother say when she knew they'd been so careless? She crouched down to peer into the boxer's stall, but all she got was a wet nose pushed into her face.

"Down, Bruno, down!" she said, impatiently. "Look – go and finish your breakfast."

"Hey – that's it!" Danny exclaimed. "If these older dogs have left some of their food, guess who'll be after it?"

"A greedy-guts puppy!" said Amy. She thumped Danny on his shoulder as if he were one of the farm animals. "Good thinking!"

Danny winced and edged away. "Yeah, well, we'd better search all these stalls."

"Wait!" warned Anna. "These are strays, they might be nervous of you. Don't go in – just look over the gates."

So they stood quietly, peering into the dim, straw-lined pens. The dogs jumped up and barked, trying to reach their visitors. The din was deafening – quite loud enough to bring Mum rushing up, thought Anna, biting her lip. Then there'd be some explaining to do!

"I can't leave him out any longer," she said, eventually. "I'd better go and tell Mum." She turned to open the main door.

"Wait a minute!" called Danny, trying to fend off the slobbering kisses of the boxer. "I think I've seen something – yes, look here!"

The girls rushed over to Bruno's stall. Danny pushed the dog's huge head aside and pointed to his feed bowl. It was empty, except for a white puppy with black and brown patches, curled up and sleeping.

"Aahhh!" said Amy. "Isn't he sweet?"

"Ohhh," groaned Anna. "How are we going to get him out? Bruno's very friendly but I wouldn't want to go into his territory."

"Joey – Joey, come on, boy," called Amy.

"That won't bring him," said Anna, crossly.

"Food might," grinned Danny. "Have you got any?"

"There's some puppy nuts in the store," said Anna.

"Right – you get a handful while I keep Bruno busy," said Danny, suddenly in charge.

"Yes – if he finds Joey in his feeding bowl he might eat him for dinner," giggled Amy.

Anna threw her an anguished look and rushed off for some puppy-nuts. While Danny kept the boxer occupied over the top of the stall gate, AnnarandAmy rattled the nuts around in a feeding bowl at the bottom. As soon as Joey heard the sound of food, he came waggling up to investigate. Swiftly, Danny bent down and hauled Joey through the gap at the bottom of the gate. He lifted him up, carefully supporting his bottom, and Joey squeaked happily and made a puddle all down Danny's sleeve!

"I should hurry up and put him back in the pen with the others," said Anna, feeling suddenly quite sick with relief. Imagine if they'd not found the puppy – what would she have told Mum?

Joey looked up at Danny out of his black-patch eye and suddenly made a lunge, licked Danny's face all over and nibbled his nose.

"Gerroff!" laughed Danny. "I'm not a puppy-nut."

"I don't know about that," said Amy. "You seem pretty nuts about puppies to me!"

Danny put the pup in with his family and closed the stall door firmly. The three of them made their way back to the farmyard, Danny and Amy chatting happily about the wonderful pups, Anna silent and still shaken.

"Seen the pups, then, Danny?" Mrs Bright called as she crossed their path.

"Oh yes," said Danny. "They're..." Anna threw him a warning look – no point worrying Mum about the escaped pup. "Just having their morning snack," he said.

Anna breathed a sigh of relief. Amy grinned.

"And you'd better go in and have yours," said Anna's mother. "Hot chocolate and hot-cross buns in the kitchen. And after that you'd better set off across the valley to Potter's Cott, if you don't want to be late."

Rufus bounded ahead of them as Anna pointed out the route down the valley and up to Potter's hill.

"Once you know the way you can easily get over here," said Amy. "You won't need a lift like I do."

"Yes – come over any time," said Anna.

"Thanks," said Danny, shortly.

They walked on in silence. Danny seemed to be getting gloomier with every step, Anna was still rather shaken after the escapade with Joey, and Amy always found the going heavy up to the ridge. When they reached the highest stile Anna turned and waved back at

Millington farmhouse, just in case her mum was looking out for them. Then they climbed over and made their way along the ridge to Potter's Cott.

Mrs Forester was waiting for them at the back gate. She was dressed in a voluminous, mud-coloured smock, spattered with paint and clay stains. Rufus dashed up to her, smiling and waving his plumed tail, but she didn't bend to pat him.

"You're early," she said, without smiling. "Had a good time, Dan?"

"Yes," said Danny, gruffly. He turned to AnnarandAmy. "Thanks," he said. "See you!" He gave Rufus a pat on his head and went into the cottage without looking back.

For some reason, Anna felt tearful again – Danny suddenly looked all lost and lonely like he did at school. She was quite relieved when Mrs Forester hustled them out of the gate.

"I'll walk back along the ridge with you," she said.

"Thank you, Mrs Forester," said Amy. "But we know the way."

"That's not the point – you never know who you might meet."

The two girls looked at her amazed. "Yes we do," said Amy. "We might meet Anna's dad on his tractor down the water meadows, and Anna's mum might come to meet us at the bridge…"

"And anyway we've got Rufus," said Anna. "He always comes with us when we're away from the farm – he's our guard dog."

Mrs Forester looked thoughtfully at Rufus, who was leading the way. "Seems good at his job," she observed. And all the way to the stile, she watched him as he dashed ahead, then came back to check they were on their way.

Danny's just like her, thought Anna. Thinks a lot, doesn't say much; it must be very quiet up at Potter's Cott. She thought of the ever-demanding animals at Millington Farm and the people who called and the stray dogs...

Rufus shoved through the bottom of the stile and bounded into the lane, barking happily now that he was on the homeward trail.

"Thank you very much for walking down with us," Anna said, shyly.

"Thank you very much for entertaining Danny," rejoined Mrs Forester. But she wasn't looking at the girls, she was watching Rufus, bounding back to round them up.

She had a very thoughtful look, Anna told herself, hopefully.

Chapter 6

The Easter holidays were always busy at Millington Farm. New lambs out on the hill, bullocks down in the meadow, and, above all, caravans and tents down by the river, arriving for the first holiday of the year. Mr Bright had an official camping site down there, and all day and every day, caravanners and campers came up the lane to the yard to fill up their water tanks and to buy eggs and milk.

"We must get Phil Weatherby up to vaccinate the puppies," Mrs Bright told Anna, as they cleaned out the stables one morning. "With all these strangers and their dogs, you never know what diseases are around."

"Will the vaccination make the pups ill?" asked Anna, anxiously.

"Oh no," her mother assured her. "Sometimes they're a bit sleepy, that's all." She surveyed the pups, milling around her feet just then. "This lot's so healthy I don't think they'll even notice," she smiled. "I'll book a house call with Phil's receptionist."

But it wasn't Phil Weatherby who called to do the vaccinations, it was his new assistant.

"Hello – Heather Barnes," she announced, taking her medical bag from her little hatchback. "Anyone at home?"

In fact, there wasn't at that moment. Anna's dad was on caravan duty down in the meadow and her mum was over at Winterspit with the Terrible Twins, as she now called the two black labradors.

"Do you know Harvey and Henry?" Anna asked the vet, as they walked up to the stables.

"Who doesn't?" she grinned. "I won't have them in the surgery, they upset every animal in the waiting room and most of the humans too. Luckily, Mr Lennox-Browne thinks I'm offering him a personal service, going out to

Winterspit every time he thinks they've got so much as a flea…"

"The Lennox-Brownes are supposed to be having two of our pups," Anna told her.

"And you're not too happy about that?" Heather looked at her closely.

"Well – you've seen what they've done to their labradors."

"Oh, don't worry about them, your mum will soon have them sorted out."

"Yes, but…" Anna hesitated. "I don't think Lisa-Jayne even wants a puppy – never mind two."

"Lisa-Jayne – she's the daughter, isn't she?"

Anna nodded. "She seems almost frightened of dogs," she said. "And she hates living in the country."

"Well, I can see those big labs would frighten anyone. They're beautiful dogs but they're well out of control. But a couple of puppies are a different matter – she might even get to like dogs once she's reared her own."

They were in the stables by now; Anna

opened up the puppies' stall and a stream of furry, feathery bodies tumbled out.

"My goodness, look at these animals!" exclaimed Heather. "Don't they look healthy?"

"Yes, they are," said Anna, feeling quite proud that she'd had something to do with their progress. "They're eating puppy-nuts every feed now."

"Good for their jaws and teeth," Heather nodded. "Now, let's see, how shall we organize this? I don't want to miss any – or to vaccinate one twice!"

"I'll pass them to you one by one," Anna suggested. "I know who's who…"

They sat side by side on an old bench with the pups rolling around at their feet. Anna took up each pup in turn and held it close, while Heather jabbed the syringe into the loose flesh around their necks.

"That's where their mother would lift them," she explained. "So it's not very sensitive. Now, who's next?"

"Last, as usual," laughed Anna, hauling Runty up to her lap. "This one was born last and is late for all his feeds…"

"Ahh, the runt of the litter!" Heather said. "Well, he's a bit small, but healthy enough." She felt him all over, checked his mouth and eyes, gave him his jab and a fond pat. "You're doing fine, little runt," she said. "Off you go, back to Mum!" She turned to Anna. "I make that six – right?"

"Right," said Anna, and she walked back to the car with Heather.

"Keep an eye on them – tell your mum to ring me if there are any unusual symptoms, but I'm sure they'll all be fine." She paused at the car door. "Sold any others?" she asked. "Apart from the two possibles?"

"Jilly – that's the mother. As soon as the pups are weaned, she's going to a lovely elderly couple with a bungalow out Cranston way." Anna looked at the young vet. "Are you interested?" she asked.

"I would be but I haven't even got a place of my own yet," she said. "It's a bit too soon to be thinking of pets." She got into the car and shut the door. "I'm sure you'll have plenty of offers now they're ready to go," she said, through the open window. " 'Bye now – see you soon, I expect."

Anna waved the vet off and then remembered she hadn't fed the geese, cleaned out the hen-house…

So it was a few hours later that she popped in to give the pups their dinner. They didn't come surging towards her as they usually did because they were still fast asleep. Obviously the effects of the vaccination hadn't worn off yet; Anna scooped them up and put them by the feeding bowls, where they soon recovered enough to slurp away happily at their scrambled eggs.

Except for one.

Runty didn't even move an eyelid as the others trod all over him. Even when Jilly gave him a push with her nose he merely gave a great sigh and went on sleeping.

Anna went across to look at him.

"Hello, Runty, old boy – are you still tired?" she whispered.

Runty didn't even wag his tail once.

Anna stroked his head and gently touched his nose end. It was warm and dry, but then, the pups' noses often were when they'd been sleeping all in a heap together. Anna stepped back and looked at the rest of the puppies dozing over their scrambled egg. Well, maybe Runty, being smaller, was just more affected by the vaccination, she thought. Even so, she'd tell her mother about Runty when she came home.

"Puppies all right?" asked Dad, when she got back to the yard.

"They're all very sleepy," she replied.

He nodded. "The effects of the vaccination, I expect," he said. "Leave them to sleep it off. Can you get a few more packs of eggs out for the campers?"

So Anna sorted eggs for the campers, showed them the tap for drinking water, pointed out the way down the lane to the camping site... She was so busy that she had no time to worry about the pups for the rest of the morning.

Mum came in from Winterspit all pink and breathless. "Heavens, those dogs are hard work," she said. "You should come over with me one day, Anna – you'd love it. Those stables – my, they're more luxurious than our house!"

"Have they got horses?" asked Anna.

"Just Mr Lennox-Browne's hunter at the moment – he's a beauty. They're getting a pony for Lisa-Jayne when they get back from holiday. What with a pony and two new pups, she's going to have her hands full." She smiled happily and switched the kettle on.

"Puppies!" exclaimed Anna. "That reminds me – the vet came to do the vaccinations…"

"Oh, good," Mum nodded. "Was Phil pleased with the pups?"

"It wasn't Phil, it was Heather Barnes, his new assistant – and Mum, the pups are awfully sleepy."

"They will be for today," smiled Mrs Bright. "They'll be back to their normal rollicking selves in the morning."

"The little one didn't even wake up for his feed," said Anna. "Not even when Jilly nudged him."

Her mother looked at her closely. "You think he wasn't well?" she asked.

"He was … what's that word Amy's grandma uses when Amy can't come to school? 'Peaky' – that's it. He looked sort of peaky." Anna waited for her mother to laugh at the description.

But she didn't.

"Right," she said. "We'd better get on up there and look at the little fellow."

Anna followed her mother up to the stables, alarmed by her swift reaction. Did she think they'd left it too late? Anna groaned inwardly: if she hadn't been so busy with the campers she might have looked in earlier and the vet had said to call if there was any change in the pups...

Her mother disappeared into the stables and Anna rushed to catch up with her. As soon as they opened the stall up, a puppy barked feebly – one had recovered, at any rate. Then another joined in, then another, until a chorus of weak, sleepy barks and yowls greeted them.

"Nothing wrong with these," commented Mrs Bright, opening up their stall. "Now, where's the little one?"

"He was close by Jilly's head," Anna told her. "I think Jilly had been licking him."

"To cool him down and comfort him," her

mother said. "You're a wonderful mother, aren't you, girl?" She bent to stroke Jilly's beautiful head. "But there's no sign of the little one now," she said, looking around.

Anna came across, stepping carefully over the heap of puppies, who were already burrowing down to sleep again. She felt about in the straw behind Jilly.

"He's here!" She bent closer and gently lifted up the inert body of the pup. "Oh, Mum, is he all right?"

"Let me see." Her mother took the pup from Anna and held him close. The puppy never moved.

It was so quiet in the stable now that Anna could hear the pup's quick, shallow breathing, like a distant insect buzzing. Her mother held him in the crook of her arm and lifted up his muzzle with her free hand. "His nose is very hot," she murmured.

"It was warm and dry when I looked," Anna said. "Oh, Mum, I should have done something…"

"You did – you told me. You couldn't have done anything more, Anna."

"But Heather said to ring if there were any problems."

"Yes, but a warm, dry nose is hardly a problem." Mrs Bright lifted up Runty's lip and looked in his mouth. "Quite pink," she said. "That's a good sign." She opened an eye but the little dog quickly pulled back and shut it again.

"Did you hurt him?" asked Anna.

"No – he doesn't seem to like the light..." Her mother thought for a moment. "Could you hold him while I just check on the others?"

"Of course," said Anna. She took the pup from her mother and held him close, aware of a rasping sound as he breathed.

The rest of the pups all greeted Mrs Bright with wagging tails, waggling bottoms and little squeaks when she stirred them up.

"They've almost recovered," said Mrs Bright. "I'll give them a few puppy-nuts and then I think we'd better take the little one down to the house with us. Keep an eye on him."

"Can I take him?" asked Anna.

"Yes – you go on ahead. I'll bring a box for him."

Anna walked carefully down to the house, trying hard not to jolt Runty. Not that he'd have cared, she thought, he was still deeply asleep. He didn't even lift his nose to the new scents in the breeze, she noticed, just lay in her arms as if...

Anna suddenly realized he might be more than asleep – he could be unconscious! Forgetting all about not jogging the pup, she quickened her pace down the path, across the yard and into the house.

"Ah, Anna – could you...?" Her dad stopped as he saw her stricken face. "What is it?" he asked.

"It's little Runty," whispered Anna, near to tears. "He's..." She couldn't go on.

"Come and sit down," said Dad, shoving a pile of egg-boxes off the sofa. "Where's Mum?"

"Here I am!" called Mrs Bright, cheerfully. "I've brought a box and a sheepskin liner. We'll bed him down on that – close to the Aga, I think." She bustled about, putting newspaper into the bottom of the box, then the sheepskin and, finally, she took the puppy from Anna and laid him in. Pushing the tabby cat aside, she placed the box on the floor by the stove. "There," she said. "Now I'm going to ring the vet."

As she was on the phone, the tabby came sniffing around the pup.

"Go back, Tabitha," said Anna. "Leave him alone!"

"No – let her stay," said Dad. "She won't hurt the pup."

So Tabitha sniffed the pup all over, then licked his ears and face, as if washing him, and eventually she eased herself into the box and snuggled down beside him.

Mrs Bright put down the phone. "Phil's not on call this weekend," she said. "But the assistant's going to look in."

"Well, I hope she comes quickly," said Anna. "Mum, do you think Tabby should stay in the box with Runty?"

Her mother regarded the two animals for a moment.

"Well, whatever's wrong with him isn't going to harm Tabby," she said. "And she's keeping him warm and comfortable. We'll leave her there until the vet comes."

It was only half-an-hour later when Anna, who'd been hovering between the yard and the kitchen, heard a car pull in.

"Mum – this is Heather Barnes." Anna introduced her as she led her into the kitchen.

"Now, where's the little chap?" asked Heather.

"Underneath the tabby cat," said Mum.

"Best place for him," grinned Heather. "Especially if he's got a bit of fever. But I need to examine the pup, not you, Tabby!"

Anna pushed Tabitha aside, picked up the box and placed it on the kitchen table. Heather didn't take Runty out, she just rolled him gently over and felt all round his body. Then she gently lifted his eyelid and peered into his eye.

"Come on, little chap," she kept saying, as she worked. "Who's a good little boy, then?"

And Anna, following the vet's every move, was thrilled to notice the smallest waggle of the tiny tail!

Heather popped the thermometer into Runty's bottom and they all waited solemnly for the result. Heather removed it and held it up to the light to check.

"Hmmmm – bit of fever, as I suspected. Not dangerous, though." She bent over and listened to his breathing. "Bit rough, that," she commented. "Bit of a sore chest, have you, lad?"

And again, Anna could have sworn she saw Runty wiggle his tail.

"Well, there's a bit of infection in the chest. Could be a reaction to the vaccine..." She went on examining the pup, peering into his mouth, gently prodding his tummy… "No, nothing internal," she said, when she'd finished. "I'll give him a shot of antibiotic and leave some pills – mash them up with his food."

"Should we keep him away from the others?" asked Mrs Bright.

"Oh, yes – he's not up to the hurly-burly of puppy life," Heather smiled. "Can he stay in here for a few days?"

"Of course," Mrs Bright said.

"What about the cat?" asked Anna.

"Best medicine out," Heather assured her. "Good mother substitute, full central heating – pup needs nothing more except a light diet and the antibiotics. Are you going to be nursing him?" She smiled down at Anna.

"Oh, I expect so," said Anna, looking over at Mum.

"Well, you're the one who said you hadn't enough to do this holiday," laughed Mum. "I'm sure your days will be full now."

Mum and Heather went out to the car, leaving Anna to put Runty back by the stove. As soon as she put the box down, Tabitha was there, snuggling on to the sheepskin liner, curling her small, neat body all round the little pup. Anna watched breathlessly as Runty snuggled closer. His little mouth twitched as if he were going to suckle, then stopped, as he fell asleep once more.

Anna stroked Tabitha's sleek little head. "We'll get him better, won't we, Tabitha?" she whispered. "You and me together!"

Chapter 7

So Anna and Tabitha took over the job of nursing little Runty. Dad was kept busy with the campers and Mum spent a lot of time up at Winterspit – she wanted to make a good start on training Harvey and Henry before the Lennox-Brownes came home from safari.

"They'll be a good advertisement for my new training course," she said. "If I ever get it off the ground." She pulled on her wax jacket. "See you at lunch-time," she told Anna. "Don't forget to feed Runty at eleven – and break a pill into his food."

Anna opened a tin of milky rice-pudding, which she scooped into Runty's mouth on her fingers. On that first frightening day he'd lain motionless in the box with Tabitha, refusing anything except dribbles of water. But now, only a day after his injection, he could lap tiny bits of food from Anna's fingers. He was still thirsty, but too weak to drink from his bowl, so Anna gave him boiled water from a baby's bottle, which they used to feed orphan lambs. And Tabitha licked his dried-up lips as she washed and groomed him hourly.

As Anna sat feeding him, Runty's eyes flickered open now and then and he even managed to waggle his tail. Anna spent the rest of the day hovering around the box by the stove, mixing rice-pudding and powdered tablets, persuading Runty to suck water from the bottle and mopping up the puddles he left at the end of his box. Tabitha left him only to eat her own food or to go out, and she quickly returned to snuggle him into her rich, golden underfur.

Of course Anna didn't forget all the other puppies. She was just coming back from a brief visit to the stables, the following afternoon, when she saw a large, expensive-looking car parked in the yard. A young man got out and wandered around, peering into the outhouses – even into the kitchen window. Anna felt a bit uneasy: her mother was still up at the stables, feeding the strays with Rufus to help her, and Dad had just gone to sort out a caravan that had jack-knifed in the lane.

"Can I help you?" she called, running down to the yard.

The man turned. "Do you live here?" he asked, smiling.

"Yes," she said. He didn't look at all like a camper, she thought, in his immaculate jeans and big leather jacket. "If you want to see Dad just ring that bell on the corner there."

"We want to see some pups, actually." An older woman got out of the car and came over to join them. His mother? wondered Anna. She too wore a leather jacket and boots, but with well-cut cords instead of jeans. "We saw you had some for sale, dear," she said, her glossy red lips parting in a smile.

"Oh, yes," said Anna, eagerly. Although she'd quite fallen in love with Runty, after six weeks of taking care of six pups she wasn't quite so keen to keep the lot of them now. "They're up in the stables."

"Can we go and look at them?" asked the young man.

Anna hesitated. There was no reason not to agree; the pups were quite old enough now for anyone to pick up and, after all, only that morning Mum had been bewailing the lack of enquiries about them.

"We'll be feeding them until they're fully grown at this rate," she'd said, opening up yet another sack of puppy-nuts.

Mum would be keen to show the pups to any interested customer, Anna decided, especially such obviously rich ones as these two. She'd already noticed the personalized number plates on the expensive car – M155 JAN – in lettering that looked like MISS JAN. These people would certainly be able to afford a good home for a puppy.

"I'll take you up there," she said, eagerly. "You can talk to Mum about it."

They followed Anna up to the stables, stepping carefully through the puddles and mud in their tan cowboy boots. Once inside, they peered over the stall door at the pile of pups in the straw.

"Mum – some people interested in the puppies," called Anna.

"Can you cope for a moment?" Her mother's voice came muffled through the back door.

"Right!" Anna turned to the visitors. "Shall

I let them out for you?" she asked.

"Not just yet," said the woman, glancing down at the wet and mess in the stall. "I can see them perfectly well from here."

Anna was surprised. Most people couldn't wait to pick one up, handle it, cuddle it and "get to know it", as they always explained.

"Five you've got?" asked the young man.

"Er, yes," said Anna. For some reason she didn't mention Runty. He wasn't fit to go with anyone yet and she didn't think Mum would want her to mention him. "Three females, two males."

"Sold any?"

"Well, I think two are promised," said Anna. "But you'd have to ask Mum about that."

The woman nodded. "Looks promising, Mike," she said to the young man.

Mike turned his charming smile on Anna. "We were thinking of three or four," he said.

"Four?" repeated Anna in amazement. How could anyone manage to bring up four pups at once? And why would they want to?

The woman obviously had the same thought. "Maybe three will be enough, after all," she said, nudging the young man hard in the back.

"What? But I thought…"

"You thought wrong," she interrupted. "Three will do just fine."

"For her grandchildren," said Mike, smiling at Anna some more.

"Oh, I see!" Anna smiled back now. What a kind grandmother, she thought – until she remembered Mum's opinion of people who gave puppies as presents.

"Might as well offer them babies," she used to say. "Same sort of cruelty."

So Anna had no doubt what her mother would say when she realized the lady wanted presents for her grandchildren. She looked anxiously along to the end door, where Mrs Bright was just emerging.

"Sorry about the delay," she smiled at the visitors. "Bit of a crisis with Bruno – boxers will eat anything, even half a brick!"

"These people are interested in the puppies," Anna told her, anxiously. She wasn't sure why, but she felt there was something not quite right. She stood back to see her mother's reaction.

"Any special one?" asked Mrs Bright, moving over to join them at the puppies' stall.

"Well now, we're great dog-lovers, aren't we, Mike?" said the woman.

"Oh yes – runs in the family," said Mike, treating Mrs Bright to one of his brilliant smiles.

Mrs Bright didn't smile back. "Good," she said. "So which pup would you like to see?"

"Pups, actually," said Mike. "We want three – could take more, but the little girl tells me you've sold a couple."

Anna flushed at his reference to her – she hated to be called "little girl".

"No – I keep telling you," the woman interrupted. "Three will be quite enough. One for each of my grandchildren." She smiled over at Mrs Bright and paused, as if expecting to be congratulated on her generosity.

Mrs Bright merely stared at her.

"How old are your grandchildren?" she asked.

The woman stalled. "Well ... heavens, it's difficult to keep count – how time flies!" She twittered on, calculating on her elegantly gloved fingers. Then, "Five, seven, nine," she said quickly.

"Mmmm." Mrs Bright was thoughtful. "I don't allow puppies to go to children, you know."

"Oh, my dear, of course not!" gushed the other woman. "They'll be properly supervised by their parents – and in beautiful homes, you know."

"That's nice," smiled Mrs Bright. "So they wouldn't mind if I paid a visit?"

"Visit?"

"Yes – I have to check the home before we allow the pups to go." She smiled very warmly. "I'll have time to do that once the holiday's over, if you'd give me their addresses…"

"Oh, but we need – we want to take them today – right now," Mike said.

Mrs Bright shook her head. "Can't be done," she told them. "They've only just had their first vaccination, I need to keep an eye on them a day or two longer…"

"That's all right," the young man interrupted. "Jan is a trained veterinary nurse –

aren't you, Jan?" He stared hard at the woman, who nodded briefly and reached into her large handbag. She took out a thick wad of notes. Anna's eyes boggled – she'd never seen so much money. "Three at – what? Fifty pounds?" the woman was saying. "Well, let's call it a couple of hundred, shall we?"

"No, we won't," said Mrs Bright, firmly. And suddenly she seemed to have made up her mind about something. "We don't let puppies go until we've done a home check," she said.

"Oh, but my dear!" drawled the woman. "You can see we're not the kind of people to neglect a dog."

Mrs Bright merely stared at her. "This is not entirely my own business, you know – we're part of a national charity. I have to guarantee that all dogs go to good homes."

"Of course you do!" soothed the young man. "But you see, Jan's family live miles away – you'd have a long way to travel to see the homes these pups are going to."

"No, we wouldn't," said Mrs Bright, and Anna was sure she saw a triumphant gleam in her eye, as if she'd just answered the last question to win a game of Trivial Pursuit. "We have representatives in all areas," she said. "I'll give them a call – they could probably do a check by the end of the week. If everything's in order, they'll ring me, I'll get the paperwork done and the pups will be ready to leave home. It all works out nicely!" Now, she too was smiling.

"But there's no need for all that, surely?" asked Jan. "You can see we're respectable people – not short of money…"

"Money's not everything when it comes to rearing puppies," said Mrs Bright, firmly. "We still need to know what kind of home they're going to."

"Two hundred and fifty pounds?" said the young man, taking a wad of notes and holding them in front of Mrs Bright's face. Anna could see now they were fifty-pound notes and there were lots of them. "And we take them straight away."

Mrs Bright shook her head. "It doesn't work like that," she said. "You can choose your pups now and I'll keep them for you.

Then, at the end of the week you come back to collect them."

"But we're only passing through," said Mike. "We live miles away."

Mrs Bright shrugged. "Oh, that's too bad," she said, though she didn't sound very sympathetic.

"It's too bad for you, lady," said the young man. "Missed a good business deal there, you have." He turned abruptly and flung open the stable door, where Rufus sat, growling loudly. Mike shoved the dog out of his way with his foot. "Come on, Jan!" he said. "No point in staying here."

Jan stared at Mrs Bright. "No wonder you're stuck here on this bit of a small-holding," she said, with a sneer. "Can't recognize a good deal when it hits you in the face." And she swept out. This time Rufus stood up, his hackles rising on his back, and barked at the departing figure.

Anna and her mother heard the car start up, swish out of the yard, and hiss down Steepy Lane far too fast. Mr Bright stood by the gate, staring angrily after the car.

Anna and her mum walked down to join him.

"Did you see that?" he asked them. "It's a good job I'd got that caravan out on the road or there'd have been a quite a smash."

"We nearly sold them three pups," Anna told him.

"What do you mean, 'nearly'?" he asked.

"Mum wouldn't let them go," Anna said.

"Not to the likes of them," said her mother. "What do you think they'd do with them?"

"Give them to the lady's grandchildren."

Mum shook her head. "Sell them in a car-boot sale, more like," she said.

"What?" Anna was horrified. "Puppies in a car-boot sale? I don't believe it."

"Oh – so that's why they were in such a hurry to get away," said Dad.

"Making a getaway," smiled Mrs Bright. And she told him all about her customers. "Anna's quite shocked, aren't you darling?" She ruffled Anna's fair hair.

"Oh, that's a well-known dodge," her dad told Anna. "Collect a few pups here, a few there – some farmers will just about give them away. Pretend you're a proper breeder and take them off to markets, car-boot sales, some are even traded along the motorways. Charge up to a hundred pounds a pup if they look like pure-breds – and you've made a handsome profit."

"But Dad – you'd never know who'd bought them, or what kind of home they'd gone to," said Anna.

"No, you wouldn't," Dad agreed. "I think I'll just give Beth Johnson a ring – she'll pass the information on to the police and to any other local kennels." He turned to his wife. "You didn't happen to get their car registration, did you?" he asked.

Mrs Bright shook her head.

"I did," said Anna. "I noticed because it was personalized and it had funny figures that made it look like MISS JAN and that was her name."

"M155 JAN," said Dad. "Well spotted, Miss Detective!"

While Dad was busy on the phone, Anna went to check on Runty. He was asleep again, snuggled almost under Tabitha's tummy. But when Anna tentatively put out a finger and touched him, he wriggled and twitched his stumpy tail. He was going to be all right, she decided, happily.

And so were the others – now they'd escaped from those dreadful puppy dealers. Anna shuddered – to think she'd been quite excited by the idea of getting rid of three puppies so easily! If those horrible people had bought them, the pups might have been driven around the markets for weeks and then sold to somebody who didn't even know how to look after them! Tears sprang into Anna's eyes as she thought about it.

She sniffed and gently stroked Runty's tiny, silken ear – until Tabitha glared at her and shifted the pup closer.

"It's all right, Tabs," she whispered to the cat. "Nobody's going to take your kitten-pup away from you." And then, as an after-thought, she crossed her fingers. "Yet," she added, sadly.

Chapter 8

"It's time that pup went back to his mother," said Dad, tipping Runty out of his wellington boot and putting him firmly back in his box.

"Oh, Dad!" protested Anna. "He's still recovering."

Tabitha stalked across the kitchen, settled herself around Runty and treated Dad to a particularly malevolent glare.

"Seems pretty healthy to me," said Dad. He held up his sock and pulled at a long strand of wool hanging from a hole in the toe. "Got a good appetite for wool, at any rate."

"It shows he's getting better," Anna said.

"It shows he's getting naughtier," said Dad.

He went into the porch and pulled on his jacket. "Seriously, Anna, it's time he went back — you're getting too attached to him."

"No, Tabitha is," smiled Anna. "Just look at the two of them now!"

Dad glanced back in the kitchen to where Tabitha had pinned the pup down in the box while she licked him all over with her rough tongue.

"She treats him like her kitten," said Anna.

"And he'll grow up thinking he's a cat," Dad pointed out. "Either he goes to a customer or to his litter before you go back to school."

Anna frowned — there were only a few days of the holidays left and she'd already begun to worry about what would happen to Runty once she was away all day. He couldn't stay in the kitchen with his beloved Tabitha, he'd never been happy with the rest of the litter and Jilly, his mother, was due to go to her new home at the weekend. Poor little Runty — he'd already had a hard life: first bullied by the rest of the litter, then being ill, and now even his own mother was going to leave him.

What on earth was she going to do about him? Anna watched the two animals settle down together, Tabitha curling her whole body around the little pup, Runty snuffling happily in search of non-existent puppy-milk, and she sighed. She desperately wanted to keep him, but she knew that once Dad made up his mind it was very difficult to shift him.

The phone suddenly shattered the silence of the kitchen. Anna ran to pick it up.

"Hi, Anna – it's Amy."

"Oh, Amy – great! Did you have a good holiday?"

"Triff!" said Amy. "And I've got the most wonderful secret to tell you."

"Well, tell me," said Anna, quite unimpressed by Amy's claim – she was a great one for "secrets" which turned out to be merely bits of village gossip everyone knew.

"No – not on the phone. Can I come over this afternoon? Gran's got to drive in to Millington, she'll give me a lift."

"Yes, and stay to tea, right?"

"Thanks – I will." There was a pause, then

Amy asked, "Have you still got some pups?"

"All of them," said Anna. "Runty's right here now."

"In the house?" Amy squeaked. "Does that mean you're keeping him?"

"Not according to Dad," said Anna. "He's been ill, you see."

"Your dad?"

"No, the pup. He's better now and Dad says he's got to go back to the stables with the others."

"And you don't want him to?"

"Of course not, I want to keep him here."

"Sounds as if you'll have a job persuading your dad," Amy observed. "And, by the way, did Danny and his mum ever come to see them?"

"No – I don't suppose he'll be back until the weekend."

"And I don't suppose his mum's given in about the puppy," said Amy, sounding, for some reason, rather smug.

Amy was probably right, thought Anna, as she washed the breakfast dishes, his mother had obviously not given way over a puppy for Danny. She looked thoughtfully down into the suds and remembered how Mrs Forester had looked at Rufus that day they'd walked up the ridge with Danny. Anna had been sure Mrs Forester was warming to the idea of a dog just then. If only Danny hadn't gone away, he might have been able to nag her into submission – though somehow, Anna didn't think Mrs Forester was the submissive type!

She sighed; the pups were ready to leave and Mum had heard from several interested people by now. What if they were all taken before Danny got back from holiday? Worse – what if Danny wanted Runty? Then again, what if neither Dad nor Mrs Forester would agree to keeping a puppy at all? Anna rubbed her nose and frowned: there were too many problems for her to solve!

"You've got foam all over your nose," said her mother, passing through the kitchen. "And I'm just off to Winterspit."

Anna stared at her. There was another problem: which pups (if any) would the Lennox-Brownes take? Well, at least they wouldn't want Runty – Mr Lennox-Browne would want the biggest and the best.

"Why don't you come over to Winterspit with me?" her mother suggested. "Harvey and Henry are quite well-behaved with me but they need to practise with a stranger. I think you're strange enough!"

"Ha ha!" said Anna. "I can't stay all day – Amy's coming round this afternoon."

"Don't worry – those dogs can't concentrate for more than half an hour," smiled Mum.

Harvey and Henry bounced out to greet them.

"Sit!" said Mum, very quietly.

And, to Anna's surprise, they both sat – for a moment. Then they were up and bouncing again.

"Sit!" said Mum. And again they sat.

"Stay!" she ordered – and this time they remained sitting, wagging their tails and wriggling their bottoms and obviously desperate to move, but just about sitting. "Good boys!" said Mum, delving into her pocket and producing two dog-biscuits. "Stay!" she said again, holding out a biscuit in either hand.

The dogs sat crunching while Mrs Bright went to collect their leads. As soon as both she and the biscuits had gone, Henry and Harvey began looking restlessly around the yard.

"Stay!" Anna said, imitating her mother's firm tone. And to her delight, they obeyed her – for a moment.

But suddenly they stood and stared over in the direction of the kitchen. Anna followed their gaze and saw Lisa-Jayne, in the doorway.

"They haven't changed," she observed, backing off as they bounded up to her. "Down! Down!" she said, helplessly.

"Oh, but they have," Anna called. "Harvey, Henry, come here!"

The dogs wheeled round and bounced back.

"Sit!" commanded Anna.

And they both sat on her feet.

"Good boys," said Anna, patting and stroking them both and holding their collars lightly.

I hope they keep still, she thought, watching Lisa-Jayne walk cautiously across the yard. Luckily, at that very moment Mrs Bright came out from the outhouse which was the kennel.

"Good boys!" she called. "Stay!" And she held out her hands, closed tight as if hiding a treat. The boys stayed with Anna.

"I don't believe it!" said Lisa-Jayne. "How did you do that?"

"I didn't," Anna admitted. "Mum did – look."

Mrs Bright came close, patted the two dogs and slipped on their halters. These were a kind of collar and lead combined, which slid behind their ears and across their noses so that they were unable to pull on the leash.

"Take one," she told Lisa-Jayne, offering her Harvey's leash. "Go on, he can't pull on that, and he's just learning to walk at heel. Heel, Harvey!" she commanded.

Lisa-Jayne reluctantly took hold of the leash and began walking. Harvey walked quietly at her side and Anna followed with Henry, who was still rather bouncy but was unable to pull because of the position of the halter.

"When you're ready, tell them to sit," called Mrs Bright. The girls did this – and the dogs sat obediently beside them. "Now, slip off their leads," said Mrs Bright. Anna took Henry's lead off, and then showed Lisa-Jayne how to slip Harvey's over his head. As soon as they felt they were free, both dogs stood up.

"Sit!" called Mrs Bright. "Stay!" She waited until the dogs were sitting once more. "Now, you two walk away," she told the girls.

Lisa-Jayne and Anna walked back to Mrs Bright, leaving the dogs still sitting there, watching them anxiously.

"Well done, boys," said Mrs Bright. "Come!" And they bounded over, exuberant as ever. But they both sat down to crunch another biscuit.

Lisa-Jayne was beaming with pride. She bent over and hugged Harvey.

"I never noticed how beautiful his coat is," she said.

"You never had a chance," said Mrs Bright. "He never stood still long enough!"

The two girls and the two dogs did a few more exercises, with Mrs Bright calling the commands. Then, to finish up, she let Lisa-Jayne take each dog in turn around the yard, giving him orders on the way. Anna could see that Lisa-Jayne was thrilled at the effect she had on the two dogs.

"Dad will never believe this," she kept saying. "Will they do this all the time, now?"

"Well, they've had enough this morning," said Mrs Bright. "Take them off to run in the paddock as a reward for their hard work."

"I think it's you who should have a reward," said Lisa-Jayne. "Mrs Binns has got coffee on in the kitchen."

"Thanks – I haven't seen Nora Binns for ages," smiled Mrs Bright. "It'll be good to have a chat with her."

The two girls stood at the paddock gate watching the dogs tearing around. Lisa-Jayne looked quite beautiful with her sun-bleached hair and tanned complexion and Anna felt suddenly rather shy of her.

But to her surprise, Lisa-Jayne suddenly asked her about the Millington puppies.

"Have you still got them?" she asked.

Pleased to find her interested, Anna told her all about Runty's illness, Joey's naughtiness and Jilly's new home.

"I expect they'll all be going to new homes very soon," she said. "Mum can't possibly cope with them when I'm back at school."

"Have you found homes for them?"

Anna shook her head. "Mum's had one or two offers but she's not happy about them," she explained.

There was a pause.

"Dad still wants me to have a couple, you know," said Lisa-Jayne.

"Well, they'd be happy with Harvey and Henry," smiled Anna. "But I thought you weren't keen?"

Lisa-Jayne hesitated. "I'm sorry I was so gloomy that day we came to your farm," she said. "I was just fed up with everything – the move, the new school, those bouncing, disobedient dogs…"

"And you feel better after your holiday?"

Lisa-Jayne's face glowed. "Oh yes," she said, rather dreamily. "And, you know, I actually missed this place – and those naughty dogs."

"They're not naughty now," Anna pointed out.

"No – that's another lovely surprise. Now I've watched your mother working I can't wait to train my own pups."

"You mean you really want them now?" asked Anna.

"Yes," smiled Lisa-Jayne. "I really do."

"Why don't you come back with us and choose them today?"

Lisa-Jayne looked at her thin gold watch. "I haven't time before my riding lesson," she said, ever so casually.

"Your riding lesson?" exclaimed Anna, sounding so amazed that Lisa-Jayne smiled.

"I know it's hard to believe," she said. "But I took a few lessons out in Kenya and my instructor said I had a natural seat."

She was blushing as she said this, Anna observed.

"Was he nice?" she asked.

"Mmmmm – quite dishy!" said Lisa-Jayne, dreamily.

"The horse?"

"Him too," laughed Lisa-Jayne. "Look, I'll get Dad to bring me over to Millington Farm tomorrow – all right?"

"All right," agreed Anna.

"And meanwhile I'll impress him by getting these two creatures back," said Lisa-Jayne. "Henry! Harvey! Here, boys!"

"Those dogs have made remarkable progress," said Mrs Bright, on the way home.

"So has Lisa-Jayne," said Anna. "She's coming to choose her puppies tomorrow."

"Oh, good, that's two gone – four to go!" said Mrs Bright. "I wonder what made her change her mind?"

"A riding instructor in Kenya," said Anna.

Her mother gave her a sharp glance – and they both burst out laughing.

Anna had been hanging over the farmyard gate for half an hour when she saw the little red sports car zooming up Steepy Lane. She clambered down and swung the gate open so that Amy's gran could pull straight into the yard.

"'Bye, Gran!" called Amy, scrambling out. "Don't forget to ring Dad to collect me on his way back from work."

"As if I would!" said her gran. "Bye Anna – must get on – lots to do!" She turned the car in an amazingly small space and, with a wave and a flourish, drove off down the lane – rather fast.

AnnarandAmy stood grinning at each other.

"Here," said Amy, thrusting out a little package. "I brought you a present from London."

"Hey, thanks. Can I open it now?"

"You'd better," smiled Amy.

But Anna waited until they were in the kitchen. She pulled open the red tissue paper to reveal a small brown box.

"Go on, open it!" urged Amy.

Anna lifted the lid off and saw a silvery brooch, in the shape of a dog's head, with a blunt, rounded snout and feather ears.

"Oh, Amy, it's lovely!" said Anna. "Just like Runty!"

"Only this one's for keeps!" said Amy. She looked across the kitchen to where Tabitha lay in a box by the fire. "Hey, is Tabitha having kittens?" she demanded.

"No – why?" Anna was busy pinning the brooch on to her sweatshirt.

"Well, Gran's cat always takes to a box when she's having kittens – and Tabitha looks amazingly bulgy."

"That's not kittens – that's Runty!" laughed Anna. "Go and see."

Amy went across to the box and pulled Runty out from Tabitha's warm embrace.

"Well – fancy that! A pup-kitten!" said Amy.

Runty squirmed down from Amy's arms and began to race around the kitchen, dribbling as he ran.

"Catch him!" called Anna. "Mum will have a fit if we have to mop up yet again."

But it was too late. Anna got the mop and bucket and cleaned the kitchen floor, while Amy cuddled the pup outside.

"Don't put him down!" called Anna. "We don't let them walk outdoors in case of infection."

"Not ever?" asked Amy.

"Not until they've had their final vacci‐
nations," said Anna, coming out to join her.
"Look, as you've got hold of him, we might as
well take him to see his brothers and sisters."

"Well, if he can settle in with a cat, he
should be all right with his litter," said Amy.

But he wasn't. Once down on the floor of
the stall, Runty cowered and trembled as the
rest of the pups scurried all over him.

"I told Dad he wasn't ready to come back,"
said Anna, tearfully. She picked him up and
held him in her arms.

"I don't think he's ever going to be ready,"
said Amy. "He prefers the company of cats."

She looked at the smallest pup thoughtfully
for a moment.

"I haven't told you my secret yet," she
observed.

"Oh, no – I was so thrilled with the brooch
I forgot all about it. Tell, tell!"

Amy watched Runty settling down in
Anna's arms. "He's like a baby," she observed.

Anna made a face. "Much nicer," she said,
decidedly.

Amy laughed. "I hope you won't think that when we get ours," she said.

"Yours?" Anna asked. "What do you mean?"

"I mean my mum's going to have a baby," said Amy. "That's the secret – isn't it wonderful?"

Anna stared at her open-mouthed. "Wonderful!" she repeated. "But what about your mum's job?"

"Well, that's the really great part. She's going to take some time out to look after the baby – and she says I can have a dog as well!"

"Amy – how marvellous – you've always wanted one. What a shame the pups came too soon…"

"But that's the great idea! If you keep a pup for me until Mum finishes work in a few weeks' time I can come and see him almost every day so we get to know each other…"

"I'm sure Mum would agree," said Anna. "And we can come up to the stables and train him after school."

"But don't you see – he wouldn't be up in the stables."

"What do you mean?" asked Anna, feeling suddenly cold.

"It's Runty I want," Amy said.

There was a pause. Anna clutched Runty close. "Why?" she whispered.

"Well, partly because he's like the baby of the litter – like our baby will be in our family," smiled Amy. "And he's got used to living in your kitchen," she added, practical as usual. "We could soon house-train him."

"But what about your gran and her cats?" said Anna, desperately.

"He's taken to Tabitha easily enough," Amy pointed out. "He'll be all right with Gran's cats and that means Gran will be all right with him. She's over the moon about the baby anyway – I'm sure she'll take to little Runty." She looked at the pup in Anna's arms. "We must think of a better name than that, though," she murmured.

Anna stared silently at her friend. How could she? How could she suggest taking Runty away from Millington Farm, away from Anna herself? Of all the pups she could have chosen, why did she have to want

Runty? She swallowed hard and tried to listen to Amy making plans.

"We'll have to talk it over with the parents, I suppose," she was going on, all business-like. "And I'd like Gran to come and see him with Tabitha — that'll convince her he's not any ordinary pup…" She chatted happily on as they walked down to the house, not noticing Anna's gloomy silence.

"Well, that's what you might call half a pup down and five-and-a-half to go," said Dad, at supper that evening.

"What do you mean?" asked Anna.

"Well, this little one's going to be AnnarandAmy's for a few weeks yet — he's not quite gone to his new home."

"And two more will be going to the Lennox-Brownes tomorrow," Mrs Bright reminded him. "So that only leaves three-and-a-half."

"I wonder who'll end up with half a pup?" smiled Dad, ruffling Anna's hair.

Anna edged away. "There's no half-a-pup," she said, irritably. "Runty will be all Amy's soon and all the rest will have gone."

"Oh, I do hope so," said her mother. "I need some time on the computer to plan my dog-training centre and Dad's got the sheep to dip and the caravan site." She laughed, happily. "It's going to be a busy summer!" she said.

Anna stared gloomily into her soup and said nothing. Of course, she told herself, the puppies had to go. She couldn't take care of them when she was back at school and they'd be growing all the time – too big for the house and too many for the stables. Yes, she could accept that, now. But after all, little Runty wasn't going to take up much room...

She sighed. "Amy wants a new name for Runty," she said, sadly.

"I'm not surprised," said Dad. "It's an awful time for a growing pup."

"We must all stop calling him Runty, from now on," said Mum. "It's not fair to make him learn the wrong name. What does Amy want to call him?"

"She can't think of anything," said Anna.

"Well, help her think up a name over the

next few days – it's the first important lesson he has to learn."

"We'll start tomorrow," said Anna.

And she suddenly felt a bit brighter. It was going to be fun sharing a puppy with Amy. He'd be living at Millington Farm for weeks yet and they'd have lots of fun together before he went off to his new home. And lots of hard work; she suddenly remembered Amy's plan to house-train him. Anna went across to the box by the stove and prodded the puppy gently.

"Come on Run – er, puppy," she said. "Time to go out for pee-pee." She turned to her mother. "That's the next important lesson he has to learn!"

Chapter 9

The Lennox-Brownes' Land Rover pulled into the yard immediately after breakfast next morning, taking the whole family by surprise.

"Heavens, he's brought his dogs!" exclaimed Mrs Bright. "I'd better get out there and head them off into the field before they start the whole stables barking."

"Good morning!" Mr Lennox-Browne greeted her. "Not too early, I hope? Only this young lady's been up since dawn, dreaming of those puppies of yours."

"That's not true, Dad," smiled Lisa-Jayne. "You were as keen as I was to come over to see them."

144

"Well, Anna will take you up," said Mrs Bright, turning to see Anna coming out of the kitchen. "I'd like to take your pair through their paces with you, Mr Lennox-Browne."

"Ah yes, I've heard all about this miracle," he said. "Question is, will they perform for me?"

"They will, if you use the same signals and movements as I do," Mrs Bright assured him. "Come on – we'll take them into Home Field."

Anna took Lisa-Jayne up to the stables, where the pups were now giving high-pitched yaps and scrambling all over one another.

"They're ready for their feed," Anna explained. "But if you want to handle them, we'd better feed them later."

She closed the outer door, then opened up the stall. The pups rolled and scattered around their feet like so many little soft toys.

"Oh – they've grown!" exclaimed Lisa-Jayne. "They look so different now. Can I hold one?"

"Of course," said Anna. "But make sure you support its bottom as you pick it up." She grabbed the first to hand and demonstrated. "Take the scruff of its neck in one hand, its bottom in the other ... ow!" Anna exclaimed, as the pup gave her a playful nip.

"Are you sure that's the right way to hold them?" laughed Lisa-Jayne.

"Oh – it is with any normal pup. This is Joey – he's a bundle of trouble."

"Well, maybe I'll give him a miss," said Lisa-Jayne. "We've had enough trouble with Dad's dogs. I fancy something gentle and quiet." She leaned down and picked up the only all-over black puppy. "Now, what's this one like?" she asked.

"Oh, she's a sweetie," said Anna. "One of the females – they're usually easier than males, especially as they get older."

"I think I'd like two females," said Lisa-Jayne, hugging the little black pup to her. "I always wanted a couple of sisters."

"Well – there's the one you've got and that one there." Anna pointed over in a corner where the black-hatted female sat, patiently waiting for the return of her sister. "They get on so well together it's a shame to part them."

"Ahh..." Lisa-Jayne crouched down and picked up the other pup. "Oh, what a lovely little white face – and those feathery ears! Oh, yes, I want these two poppets, I really do."

So Anna shooed the other three back into the stall and led the way out.

"I'd better carry one for you," she said, taking the black pup from Lisa-Jayne. "They wriggle so – and they're not allowed to be on the ground out here."

"But they'll be all right at home?"

"Oh yes – indoors or in your courtyard. Can't go out in public until the last vaccination, in three months."

"Oh, I shan't want them to go anywhere without me," said Lisa-Jayne, happily. "I wonder what I should call them?"

Lisa-Jayne sat in the front of the Land Rover, arms full of puppy, while Anna went over and rang the bell as a signal to her mother, who eventually came back alone.

"I've left your father practising commands," she explained to Lisa-Jayne. "Are those the two you want?" she smiled.

"Oh, yes, please. Anna tells me they're good

sisters so I think they'll get on well."

"Have you got everything you need for two new pups?" asked Anna.

"Harvey and Henry were pups last year," Lisa-Jayne reminded her. "We've still got lots of their things – baskets, bedding, collars… I spent yesterday finding and washing them."

"Well, provided you put Harvey and Henry into the back of the Land Rover, and you sit with the pups, I see no reason why you can't take them home today," said Mrs Bright. "They've not been fed yet so they shouldn't be sick on the way. I'll just go and get all the documents and a bag of puppy feed to start you off…"

Anna stood watching Lisa-Jayne holding the two puppies on her lap.

"I'll fetch you an old towel in case of accidents," she said.

Lisa-Jayne smiled. "I've brought one – in the back. Could you pass it to me?"

So Anna wrapped the puppies in a fluffy, dark-blue towel, which looked as if it had just been taken straight from the bathroom cupboard rather than the rag-heap. Lucky puppies! she thought, going to such a lovely home! She didn't mind in the least that these two puppies were going now. It was so right that they would be together, and Lisa-Jayne was obviously going to treat them well.

"I'm going to call this one Gemma, after my best friend back home." Lisa-Jayne was holding up the white-faced pup. "That's a pretty name for a pretty lady, isn't it?"

"Yes, it is," agreed Anna. "Gemma – there you are, Gemma!" She stroked the puppy's black-capped head.

"I need a twinny sort of name for the other," mused Lisa-Jayne. "Something beginning with J..."

"How about Jet, as she's so black?" suggested Anna.

"Mmmm – Gem and Jet – they go well together."

"Or even Gemma and Jetta," suggested Anna.

"Yes – that's it – Gemma and Jetta – twin sisters with twin names."

The two girls spent the next few minutes repeating the names over and over again, convincing themselves that the puppies were already responding. Then Mrs Bright emerged with various papers and an exhausted-looking Mr Lennox-Browne.

"I must say, Laura, you've done wonders with these dogs," he said. He opened up the back of the Land Rover and ordered Harvey and Henry inside. "Sit, boys!" he commanded – and they sat, grinning happily out of the window with half-a-yard of pink tongue dangling. "I hope you'll give this new pair a few lessons," he added, peering at the bundle in Lisa-Jayne's arms. "You should open up a training school, you know."

"I'm hoping to," smiled Mrs Bright. "But it won't be this year – we've no funds to spare for a new project just now."

Mr Lennox-Browne looked thoughtful. "Come and talk to me when you've worked out a business plan," he said.

"Thanks – I'll do that," said Mrs Bright.

She and Mr Lennox-Browne leaned against the bonnet, sorting through the puppies' papers, while Anna climbed up beside Lisa-Jayne and took Jetta on her lap. The two girls cuddled the pups, and told them their names over and over again until they snuggled up on their shoulders and dozed off. From the back of the Land Rover, Harvey and Henry watched with great interest and surprising calm.

"Right – off we go, then," said Mr Lennox-Browne, opening the driver's door. "Ring me soon about the training school idea," he told Mrs Bright. "And I'll ring you about these pups if they don't behave themselves!" He helped Anna down from the driving seat. "Do you train daughters too?" he asked jovially.

"Dad! I'm the best-trained daughter you've got," laughed Lisa-Jayne, peering out from a collar of puppies.

Anna and her mother waved them goodbye and turned to go into the farmhouse.

"They're going to a good home – and we'll probably be seeing them again if they get as out of hand as Harvey and Henry did."

"You'll soon sort them out," said Anna.

Her mother looked down at the cheque in her hand. "Well, those two naughty dogs did me a very good turn," she said. "I'll put this away in our holiday fund."

"Can we really go on holiday this year?" asked Anna. Holidays were always difficult on the farm — it was always harvest or planting season, or lambing or sheep dipping, and even if things were quiet on the land they had too many animals to leave.

"Well, Amy's mum has offered to run the sanctuary for a week while she waits for the baby to arrive, so if Dad can get some help with the livestock I think we could get away just for a week."

"How about a safari in Kenya?" grinned Anna.

"More like a week in Cornwall with Gran," laughed her mother. "Now, what about the three pups up in the stables? It's well past their feeding time."

It was strange feeding only three pups, Anna thought, as she tried to share out the puppy-meal into three exact piles.

"Come on, you little lot!" she called, opening up the stable door. "Now, who've we got left?"

There was the badger one, with a stripe

down his face, the freckly one Amy used to like so much, and, of course, the clown, with the patch on his eye – Joey. He careered forwards and fell into his heap of food, got up and immediately scrambled over to take the freckly pup's share.

"Oh, Joey – you're so naughty," laughed Anna. "You'll need Mum's training course when you grow older." She brightened at the thought – perhaps he'd be so naughty he'd have to stay at Millington Farm!

Anna was busy cleaning out the stall – helped not at all by Joey, who had fallen in love with her broom and was determined to take it to his bed – when the stable door opened and her mother called out.

"Anna – are the pups safe? Can we come in?"

Visitors to see the pups! As usual, Anna's heart sank even though she knew in her head that this was the right thing to do.

"Yes – they're in the stall with me," she called back. Wiping her hands down her jeans, she stood up to peer over the half-door and saw Mrs Forester approaching.

"Hello, Anna," she said, in her usual serious manner. "I hear you've got some pups for sale."

Anna saw she had Danny at her side.

"Hi, Anna," he said, casually. "We've come to choose a dog or two." Then his face split into a huge grin. "Can we come in?" he said.

"I'll let them out, if you like," she offered, beaming back at him. "There's only three left now."

She opened up the half-door and the three pups scuttled out, clambering all over Danny's trainers and tugging at his laces.

"Hey – where's that little one we called Runty?" asked Danny.

Anna hesitated. Danny was bound to be hurt when he knew where Runty was going.

"He's in our kitchen," she said. "He's been ill."

Danny grinned. "I knew you'd be keeping him."

"Oh no – worse luck!" said Anna. Then she went on – because he was bound to find out sooner or later – "Amy's having him."

"Is she really?" Danny sounded interested

but not upset, Anna noticed. "But what about her gran's cats?"

"Oh, he's been living with our cat more than a week now and he loves her. He thinks he's a kitten!"

"Well, I'd rather have a pup who knows he's a dog," declared Danny.

"So what are you looking for?" asked Mrs Bright. "We've got two males and a female left."

"What do you advise?" asked Mrs Forester. "This is the first time we've had a dog."

"Dogs," Danny corrected her. "We want one for the country – here with Mum – and one for the town, for Dad. Then I'll have a dog wherever I'm staying."

"Lucky you!" exclaimed Mrs Bright. "But I can't let a puppy go to someone who's out at work all day."

"Oh, Dad works at home," said Danny.

"He's a designer," explained Mrs Forester, quickly. "He has his office in the flat."

"Ah, well, that's all right, then," smiled Mrs Bright. "Well, maybe you'd like one male, one female?"

"A male for Mum, a female for Dad?" Danny suggested.

The two women laughed.

"I do think a female might be better in town," said Mrs Bright. "Does your dad live near a park or a river where he can take her for walks?"

"Oh yes. Richmond Park is huge, like a chunk of countryside," said Danny. "And Dad lives close to the gates."

He bent down and picked up the stripey pup.

"I remember you – that day when we lost Joey," he said. "Badger, I called you, and it's just the right name." He looked over at his mother. "Can we have this male?" he asked.

"Which is the female?" asked Mrs Forester, rather nervously.

Anna picked up the freckly dog. "She's a poppet," she said, handing her over. "Just support her bottom – she always sits quite still, not as wriggly as some we have." She looked down at Joey.

Mrs Forester was looking down into the pup's eyes. The pup was looking up at Mrs

Forester, utterly calm and trusting.

"Well, you're certainly a right bonny lass," murmured Mrs Forester. "I could take to you all right."

"Do you think Dad will take to her?" asked Danny. "Or would he be better with Badger?"

His mother hugged the freckly puppy close to her and bent her head so that her face was hidden. "I don't know," she muttered.

"Maybe he'll have to come down here and find out," suggested Danny, hopefully.

There was a silence in the stables for a moment, broken only by the whimpering of the strays and the snuffling of the puppies. Danny Forester and his mother each hugged their pups close and said nothing.

Suddenly loud squeals broke out from floor-level – Joey had got himself stuck underneath the outer door.

"This one's going to be a bundle of trouble for somebody!" said Mrs Bright, pulling the fat pup from underneath the door. "I certainly don't think he's suitable for a first-time owner. Stick to the quiet female and the big, placid male. I think you'll be all right

with them." She paused as if searching for the right words. "And after all, if you have any problems, we're only just across the valley, aren't we?"

"Badger and Bonnie," announced Danny, suddenly. "That's it Mum, isn't it?"

His mother lifted her head and looked steadily at him.

"That's it, then, Danny," she said. Her face suddenly lit up with a huge smile. "Tell you what – we'll ask Dad over to meet them and then decide where they're going to live."

And Anna had the feeling that they'd be deciding on a lot more than a home for the pups.

"Can you give me a list of equipment and food?" Mrs Forester asked Anna's mum. "I'm so new to this game I don't think we've anything suitable up at Potter's Cott."

"Oh – cardboard boxes are best to start with. Lots of newspapers and an old sweater or two, a safe haven where they can be shut in when you're not about, and I'll give you the first few days' food. The rest you'll collect soon enough. Look, come down to the house and we'll sort it all out over a coffee – Anna and Danny can bring the pups."

Anna shut Joey into Jilly's stall so that he wouldn't be all on his own. She carried Bonnie down to the house, with Danny bearing Badger as if he were made of glass, and they all settled around the kitchen table to sign the papers and find books on dog-rearing for Mrs Forester.

"Come over and help us with them any time," she told Anna.

"Amy's having this one." Anna indicated Runty, who was cowering in his box, sheltered by Tabitha. "So once they've had their final vaccinations we could train them all together in our field, like a puppy school."

"You'll have to train Danny and me, too," smiled Mrs Forester.

"And Dad, when he comes over," Danny reminded her.

"Yes, and Dad as well," she agreed, quietly.

"That's what I call a good day's work," said Anna's dad, when he came in for his dinner, reeking of sheep-dip.

"Not as good as ours, I'll bet," said Mrs Bright. "Only one-and-a-half pups to go."

"Is that all? Well done!" Mr Bright tweaked Anna's hair. "And you're happy about it all, Anna?" he asked.

"Oh, yes," smiled Anna. "You see, all the pups are going to be living quite close. I'll be able to watch them growing up."

"Except for the one Danny's dad is taking back to town," her mother pointed out.

"*If* he takes him back to town," said Anna. "Somehow, I think he'll be coming back here to see his dog rather than taking it to town."

"Well, they'll be happier in the country – and happier together, I think," said Mrs Bright.

"Don't you think Mr and Mrs Forester might be happier together?" asked Anna.

Her mother shook her head. "I don't know either of them," she pointed out. "And neither do you. We might be able to make up happy endings for the pups but human beings are quite a different matter."

It would be nice, Anna thought, as she washed the dinner dishes later, if Danny's dad did come to stay at Millington. Then Badger and Bonnie could stay together, and Danny and his mum and dad would be together. She smiled at the idea. Anna liked things all neat and tidy.

Chapter 10

They were making Jilly nice and tidy, ready for her new owners, when Anna suddenly realized this left them with one last problem.

"What about Joey?" she asked. "He can't stay here all on his own."

Her mother sighed. "You're right," she admitted. "I think we'll have to move him…"

"He could come to the kitchen, with Run… the little one."

"And get out every time we opened the door? He's a runner, that one!"

Anna had to admit this was true. "So where shall we put him?"

"Well, the other pup needs a safe place now

that it's warm enough to leave the kitchen door open all day. Why don't we make up a kennel for them both in the old wash-house?"

"That's a great idea!" said Anna. The wash-house was right next to the kitchen so it would be almost as good as having Joey at home. "I'll get Amy to come and help!"

Amy's grandma brought her over and stayed to check upon the famous pup who thought he was a kitten. She was amazed to see him curled up in his box with Tabitha – and even more surprised when the cat stirred him up and led him out to squat in the yard.

"Well, who would have believed it!" she exclaimed. "It just goes to show how intelligent cats are." She bent to stroke Tabitha, who was holding down the puppy whilst she cleaned him all over. "Oh, he's a little sweetie – what's his name?" she asked.

There was a pause. Anna looked at Amy. Amy looked around for inspiration.

"I don't know," she admitted. "I'm thinking about it."

"Well, you can think while we're making a

new home for him," said Anna. "He's going to share it with the last puppy – the one with the clown patches."

"Oh – Joey, the naughtiest one," said Amy. "I hope they get on together."

"I hope he doesn't teach our pup any naughty tricks," said Gran.

AnnarandAmy looked at one another and smiled. "Our pup," Gran had said – she obviously approved!

They worked all morning, sweeping out the little wash-house, fetching a couple of hay-bales down and fixing a barrier so that the pups could be safe even when their door was open. By lunch time the kennel was ready, so Amy fetched her unnamed pup and Anna went up to the stables to collect Joey the clown. Jilly had gone now and as soon as Anna opened up the stall Joey was shoving his little fat body under the gap in the stable door. Luckily his body was just too fat! Anna hauled him up and carried him, wriggling and protesting, down to his new home.

"Whew!" she exclaimed, almost dropping

him into the hay. "He's so strong, that dog, I can hardly hold him even now!"

"He'll need a strong owner then," said Amy. "I wonder who'll take him?"

"I don't know," said Anna. "Mum says he'll have to go to someone with a firm hand."

"Like she has?" smiled Amy.

Anna groaned. "Don't!" she said. "I've suggested that but she'll never agree."

They fed the pups rice-pudding for lunch. The littlest pup of them all lapped as delicately as any kitten whilst Joey gulped his down in seconds then rolled in the dish.

"Joey and his coat of many colours," laughed Anna, picking up the puppy and mopping him with a bit of old towel.

"That's Joseph – in the bible story," Amy corrected her. "We did it last term – and we went to see that musical at the comprehensive school, remember?"

"Of course – *Joseph and his Technicolour Dream Coat*!" said Anna. "So Joey's got the right name after all."

"Only if his new owners like it," Amy reminded her. She picked up her own puppy and held him close. "I just wish I could find the right name for this little one."

"He's the baby of the litter," said Anna. "What about Babe?"

Amy made a face. "He was a pig," she said, indignantly. "I'm not giving my pup a pig's name."

"What was the name of Joseph's youngest brother in the Bible story?" Anna asked.

"That was Benjamin," said Amy. She suddenly looked up at Anna and beamed. "Benjy!" she exclaimed. "That's a nice doggy sort of name."

"Joseph and Benjamin, devoted brothers," declared Anna.

And so they were for one split second. Then Joseph made a sudden leap on to Amy's lap – and on top of his little brother, Benjamin, who cowered back and squealed.

"Now then, Joey!" said Anna, prising him away. "You're supposed to be kind to your youngest brother."

"I don't think he's read the story," giggled Amy.

*   *   *

When school started again, Joey and Benjy were still sharing their "kennel". Annarand-Amy cleaned it out every afternoon after school and spent a long time playing with the two dogs, and nobody mentioned finding a home for Joey. Anna held her breath and waited.

Danny, too, was holding his breath. His dad had been over to see the pups and had decided they should stay at Potter's Cott until their final vaccination. Meanwhile, he was so keen to get to know them that he came back every weekend – much to Danny's delight. And, Anna suspected, to Mrs Forester's too.

"But what will you do after their vaccination?" Amy asked him with her usual bluntness.

Danny shrugged. "I don't know," he admitted. "I don't want either of them to go."

And Anna sympathized with him: she didn't want Joey, the last remaining pup, to go but she had the feeling that her mother would get rid of him after his final vaccination.

On vaccination day Heather Barnes came over to Millington Farm.

"I had to check on that lame heifer," she explained, "so I thought I'd save you a journey – the vaccine's in my bag. Where are the pups?"

"In their own little house," said Anna. "This way." She led the vet to the wash-house.

"Are you going to hold yours?" she asked Amy.

Amy swallowed hard and turned rather pale. "You do it," she said, handing Benjy over to Anna.

Anna set the pup on top of the covered water-butt. She held him quite still as Heather plucked up the loose flesh on his neck and plunged the needle in. Amy turned her back until it was all over, then she picked up Benjy and held him close.

"Poor little boy!" she murmured. "Did it hurt you, then?"

"No it didn't!" laughed Heather Barnes. "I'm quite well-known for my painless injections."

Joey, of course, was quite different. Anna stood him up three times before he actually stayed still enough for Heather to get a grip on him.

"My – he's a strong character!" she exclaimed. "I could do with one like him now I've found a cottage. Is he still for sale?"

"Yes, he is," said Anna, glumly.

"What's up – don't you want to part with him?" smiled Heather.

"Not yet," said Amy, from the kennel doorway. "They're such good friends we don't want to part them."

Heather looked at the two pups, now rolling around play-fighting quite happily.

"Tell you what," she said. "I'll leave him here while I get my cottage all settled. Then why don't we give them both a great sendoff? How about a Puppy Party for them all?"

"What do you mean?" asked Anna.

"Well, I'm going to start a Puppy Playgroup up at the surgery and I'd like to try out a few ideas first. I could use the farewell party as a rehearsal for the regular thing."

"Oh, that's a great idea!" said Amy. "Could it be in a couple of weeks so I can take Benjy home afterwards?"

Great idea! thought Anna, gloomily. After the party there'd be no puppies left at Millington Farm. Still, she consoled herself, it would be lovely to see them all together again.

On half-term Saturday, Millington Farm yard was crammed with cars and vans – and the Lennox-Brownes' shining new Land Rover. People milled about, coaxing puppies to show off their lead-training, comparing their progress with the rest.

"Oh yes, he knows his name. Comes to call every time, don't you, Badger... Badger... Badger – come here, boy!" Mrs Forester called the pup, who blithely ignored her.

"Been dry and clean for two weeks now, haven't you, darling Jetta?" Lisa-Jayne was saying. "Well – nearly," she added, as the pup made a puddle on Mrs Forester's boot.

"Don't mind me!" she laughed. "Ours haven't a clue!"

Heather Barnes had set up an adventure playground in the back yard of the stables, with tyres and tunnels and huge boxes for the

pups to play in. As soon as they arrived, they strained at their various leashes, getting thoroughly mixed up and tangled.

"That's the first party-game," laughed Heather. "Pass the dog-lead!"

Once the pups were released and playing wildly with the "toys", their owners relaxed with drinks and refreshments, which Annar- andAmy had brought up earlier and Danny helped to pass round. Danny usually went to stay with his dad in the holidays but this time his dad had come to stay at Potter's Cott.

"Which pup will your dad take back to town?" Amy asked, not so innocently.

Danny blushed. "He wants them both to stay here," he said.

"Oh, what a shame – he won't have a dog at home!" Amy was full of pity for anyone who had no dog.

"He hasn't even got a home, now," Danny said. "He's doing a project for a firm in the Midlands, so he's given up the flat in Surrey."

"So you'll have two dogs up at Potter's Cott?" asked Anna.

"And two parents, apparently." Danny

grinned. "Those dogs have worked miracles," he said. "They seem to have made everyone happy."

Except me, thought Anna, turning to watch the puppies cavorting wildly around the yard. Everyone was happy with their pups and the pups were obviously very happy in their new homes – they didn't need Millington Farm any more. They didn't need her.

Her gloomy thoughts were interrupted by Heather Barnes, calling all owners to join her in the yard.

"I'm going to do a bit of training – in a playful way," she said. "Could you put your puppy on the lead?" She turned to Anna. "I'll take Joey as a demonstration model," she smiled.

"He's not very good at it," Anna said, doubtfully.

"He will be," said Heather, confidently.

Soon, everyone had a puppy at the end of a lead: Danny and his dad took Badger and Bonnie, Lisa-Jayne and Anna took Jetta and Gemma, Amy had her Benjy and out in front, Joey rolled and struggled and fought at

Heather's feet.

But Heather wasn't perturbed. She set Joey upright – several times – and showed the others how to walk the puppies right at their heel on a short leash, pausing to teach them "sit" now and then. Lisa-Jayne's two were already perfectly trained to this and she basked in Heather's compliments. The others did a bit then forgot and started to pull but were soon corrected. Except for Joey, who continued to chafe and roll and bite and growl as if it were all a great game.

"Thank you, Joey – you've just proved the point that vets make the worst dog-trainers!" laughed Heather. "I can see I'll have to put in a lot of work with this one!"

The pups were let loose again, to scramble amongst the puppy feed which Mrs Bright now scattered all around as their party food.

Finally, they were collected and rewarded with a party-bag of chews, and people began to move off to their cars. For once Amy was eager to get home – this time with Benjy. Her gran had been so impressed with his cat-like behaviour that she'd offered to look after him until Amy's mum finished work.

"I'll bring him back very often," she promised Anna. "We'll train him together – right?" She looked anxiously over Benjy's head at her friend.

"Right," Anna smiled. "You know, ever since you gave him a new name he's grown as big and strong as all the others – he's not at all runty any more!"

And it was true, she reflected, later, as she cleared up the party litter from the stables. The old Runty was gone for good, now – and all those helpless, squirming, wriggling little puppies born in the top stall many weeks ago. Now they were all grown and gone! Anna sighed, sad at the thought of losing them, yet glad that they'd all got such good homes. And so close to Millington Farm she'd be able to see each and every one of them growing up! Smiling now, she shoved the last of the party debris into a black plastic sack and carried it down to the farmyard.

Heather Barnes was taking a travel cage out of the back of her car.

"Are you going to help me persuade Joey to

get into this thing?" she smiled. "I'll bet it takes two of us."

"Yes – all right." Anna put down the sack. "Shall I hold him while you open up the cage?"

She took Joey into her arms and held him tightly. As usual he fought and struggled – this time so fiercely she had to let him go.

"Oh!" she cried. "He's running away. Stop him!"

But Joey was already squeezing under the gate into Top Meadow. Heather dropped the travel-case and raced along with Anna, over the gate and into the meadow. Joey thought this was a great game and it was some time before they could corner him. Heather picked him up this time – by the scruff of his neck – pushed him firmly over one shoulder and carried him back to the car.

"You open the cage," she told Anna. "I'll get him in."

Finally, the battle over, Joey was safely enclosed in the dog-cage, chewing madly on his "good-boy biscuits".

"Though what he's done to earn it, I don't

know," laughed Heather.

She turned and looked serio
for a moment.

"He'll make a good guard dog for my house
and for my car when I'm out on my rounds,"
she said. "And you'll see him quite often," she
added. "He'll be with me when I come over to
the livestock on the farm. And Laura and I
are making plans for the Puppy Playgroup to
be held here – you've got a much better area
for it than I have…"

Anna smiled, feeling suddenly very happy.
"I'm glad he's going to you, Heather," she
said. "That means all six pups live close by
and I'll see them quite often." She pushed a
finger through the cage bars and waggled at
the little pup. "Try to be a good boy, Joey,"
she said. Joey merely grinned, grabbed her
finger and chomped on it.

"Ow!" cried Anna.

"Personally, I'd stick to your Rufus," said
Heather, bending to pat the farm dog. "He's
got such good manners!"

She shut Joey into the back of the car, and
prepared to drive off.

...myard gate and watched ... Lane – the sixth and last ... all was quiet on Millington Fa... ..., she didn't feel at all sad now it had hap...ned. They'd all be coming over to Heather's playgroup, maybe even to Mrs Bright's new training school, which she was setting up with Mr Lennox-Browne's backing. And there'd be other pups and other dogs arriving and departing all the year round. Anna smiled ruefully – would she ever learn not to get attached to them?

Meantime, the resident strays would be waiting to be taken for a run, to be fed, to be cleaned out...

"Come on, Rufus!" Anna called. "Let's get to work!"

If you like animals, then you'll love
Hippo Animal Stories!

Thunderfoot
Deborah van der Beek
When Mel finds the enormous, neglected horse
Thunderfoot, she doesn't know it will change her
life for ever...

Vanilla Fudge
Deborah van der Beek
When Lizzie and Hannah fall in love with the same dog,
neither of them will give up without a fight...

A Foxcub Named Freedom
Brenda Jobling
An injured vixen nudges her young son away from her.
She can sense danger and cares nothing for herself – only
for her son's freedom...

Pirate the Seal
Brenda Jobling
Ryan's always been lonely – but then he meets Pirate
and at last he has a real friend...

Animal Rescue
Bette Paul
Can Tessa help save the badgers of Delves Wood
from destruction?

Midnight Dancer
Elizabeth Lindsay

Ride into adventure with Mory and her pony,
Midnight Dancer

Book 1: Midnight Dancer
Mory is thrilled when she finds the perfect pony. But will
she be allowed to keep her?

Book 2: Midnight Dancer: To Catch a Thief
There's a thief with his eye on Mory's mother's sapphire
necklace – and it's down to Mory and Midnight Dancer
to save the day...

Book 3: Midnight Dancer: Running Free
Mory and Dancer have a competition to win. But they
also have a mystery to solve...

Book 4: Midnight Dancer: Fireraisers
There's trouble on Uncle Glyn's farm – because there's a
camper who loves playing with fire. Can Mory and
Dancer avert disaster?

Look out for:

Book 5: Midnight Dancer: Joyriders
Book 6: Midnight Dancer: Winners and Losers

Hippo Fantasy

Lose yourself in a whole new world, a world where anything is possible – from wizards and dragons, to time travel and new civilizations... Gripping, thrilling, scary and funny by turns, these Hippo Fantasy titles will hold you captivated to the very last page.

The Night of Wishes
Michael Ende

Malcolm and the Cloud-Stealer
Douglas Hill

The Crystal Keeper
James Jauncey

The Wednesday Wizard
Sherryl Jordan

Ratspell
Paddy Mounter

Rowan of Rin
Rowan and the Travellers
Emily Rodda

The Practical Princess
Jay Williams

The Babysitters Club

Need a babysitter? Then call the Babysitters Club. Kristy Thomas and her friends are all experienced sitters. They can tackle any job from rampaging toddlers to a pandemonium of pets. To find out all about them, read on!

1. Kristy's Great Idea
2. Claudia and the Phantom Phone Calls
3. The Truth About Stacey
4. Mary Anne Saves The Day
5. Dawn and the Impossible Three
6. Kristy's Big Day
7. Claudia and Mean Janine
8. Boy-Crazy Stacey
9. The Ghost At Dawn's House
10. Logan Likes Mary Anne!
11. Kristy and the Snobs
12. Claudia and the New Girl
13. Goodbye Stacey, Goodbye
14. Hello, Mallory
15. Little Miss Stoneybrook ... and Dawn
16. Jessi's Secret Language
17. Mary Anne's Bad-Luck Mystery
18. Stacey's Mistake
19. Claudia and the Bad Joke
20. Kristy and the Walking Disaster
21. Mallory and the Trouble With Twins
22. Jessi Ramsey, Pet-Sitter
23. Dawn On The Coast
24. Kristy and the Mother's Day Surprise
25. Mary Anne and the Search For Tigger
26. Claudia and the Sad Goodbye
27. Jessi and the Superbrat
28. Welcome Back, Stacey!
29. Mallory and the Mystery Diary
30. Mary Anne and the Great Romance
31. Dawn's Wicked Stepsister

32. **Kristy and the Secret Of Susan**
33. **Claudia and the Great Search**
34. **Mary Anne and Too Many Boys**
35. **Stacey and the Mystery Of Stoneybrook**
36. **Jessi's Babysitter**
37. **Dawn and the Older Boy**
38. **Kristy's Mystery Admirer**
39. **Poor Mallory!**
40. **Claudia and the Middle School Mystery**
41. **Mary Anne Vs. Logan**
42. **Jessi and the Dance School Phantom**
43. **Stacey's Emergency**
44. **Dawn and the Big Sleepover**
45. **Kristy and the Baby Parade**
46. **Mary Anne Misses Logan**
47. **Mallory On Strike**
48. **Jessi's Wish**
49. **Claudia and the Genius Of Elm Street**
50. **Dawn's Big Date**
51. **Stacey's Ex-Best Friend**
52. **Mary Anne and Too Many Babies**
53. **Kristy For President**
54. **Mallory and the Dream Horse**
55. **Jessi's Gold Medal**
56. **Keep Out, Claudia!**
57. **Dawn Saves The Planet**
58. **Stacey's Choice**
59. **Mallory Hates Boys (and Gym)**
60. **Mary Anne's Makeover**
61. **Jessi and the Awful Secret**
62. **Kristy and the Worst Kid Ever**
63. **Claudia's ~~Freind~~ Friend**
64. **Dawn's Family Feud**
65. **Stacey's Big Crush**
66. **Maid Mary Anne**
67. **Dawn's Big Move**
68. **Jessi and the Bad Babysitter**
69. **Get Well Soon, Mallory!**
70. **Stacey and the Cheerleaders**
71. **Claudia and the Perfect Boy**
72. **Dawn and the We Love Kids Club**
73. **Mary Anne and Miss Priss**
74. **Kristy and the Copycat**
75. **Jessi's Horrible Prank**
76. **Stacey's Lie**

Goosebumps

R.L.Stine

Reader beware, you're in for a scare!
These terrifying tales will send shivers up your spine:

1	**Welcome to Dead House**
2	**Say Cheese and Die!**
3	**Stay out of the Basement**
4	**The Curse of the Mummy's Tomb**
5	**Monster Blood**
6	**Let's Get Invisible**
7	**Night of the Living Dummy**
8	**The Girl Who Cried Monster**
9	**Welcome to Camp Nightmare**
10	**The Ghost Next Door**
11	**The Haunted Mask**
12	**Piano Lessons Can Be Murder**
13	**Be Careful What You Wish For**
14	**The Werewolf of Fever Swamp**
15	**You Can't Scare Me**
16	**One Day at Horrorland**
17	**Why I'm Afraid of Bees**
18	**Monster Blood II**
19	**Deep Trouble**
20	**Go Eat Worms**
21	**Return of the Mummy**
22	**The Scarecrow Walks at Midnight**
23	**Attack of the Mutant**
24	**My Hairiest Adventure**
25	**A Night in Terror Tower**
26	**The Cuckoo Clock of Doom**
27	**Monster Blood III**
28	**Ghost Beach**
29	**Phantom of the Auditorium**
30	**It Came From Beneath the Sink!**
31	**Night of the Living Dummy II**
32	**The Barking Ghost**
33	**The Horror at Camp Jellyjam**

**Reader beware – here's THREE TIMES
the scare!**

**Look out for these bumper GOOSEBUMPS
editions. With three spine-tingling stories by
R.L. Stine in each book, get ready for three
times the thrill ... three times the scare ...
three times the GOOSEBUMPS!**

GOOSEBUMPS COLLECTION 1
Welcome to Dead House
Say Cheese and Die
Stay Out of the Basement

GOOSEBUMPS COLLECTION 2
The Curse of the Mummy's Tomb
Let's Get Invisible!
Night of the Living Dummy

GOOSEBUMPS COLLECTION 3
The Girl Who Cried Monster
Welcome to Camp Nightmare
The Ghost Next Door

GOOSEBUMPS COLLECTION 4
The Haunted Mask
Piano Lessons Can Be Murder
Be Careful What You Wish For

The CAFÉ Club

Make room for a delicious helping of the Café Club and meet the members; Fen, Leah, Luce, Jaimini, Tash and Andy. Work has never been so much fun!

1: GO FOR IT, FEN!

Fen and her friends are fed up with being poor. Then Fen has a *brilliant* idea – she'll get them all jobs in her aunt's café! Surely parents and homework won't get in the way of the Café Club...

2: LEAH DISCOVERS BOYS

Leah's got plenty to occupy her – there's the Café Club, home-work and the Music Festival. She certainly hasn't got time for boyfriends... But when her music teacher starts picking on her, help arrives in the form of a surprisingly attractive *boy*...

3: LUCE AND THE WEIRD KID

Nothing's working out for Luce at the moment. Grounded ... with *purple* hair ... and now this weird kid's got her into deep trouble at the café...

4: JAIMINI AND THE WEB OF LIES

Sometimes Jaimini wishes she weren't so clever. Then her parents wouldn't want to *ruin* her life by sending her to a posh school away from her friends. But as the Café Club plot to save her, Jaimini meets Dom and begins to change her mind...